THE GREAT RESET

[CTRL+ALT+HUMAN]

JUAN ANTONIO MARCH

Vitasta

Published by
Renu Kaul Verma
Vitasta Publishing Pvt Ltd
4348/4C, Ansari Road, Daryaganj
New Delhi - 110002
info@vitastapublishing.com

ISBN: 978-81-991712-5-1

First Edition 2025

MRP ₹495

Layout by Shubhpreet Kaur
Cover Design by Smriti Maheshwari
Printed by Vikas Computer and Printers, New Delhi

To my two children, Milena and Alexander, the two people in their early twenties who encouraged me to write this book, trusting that their generation can make it true.

This work, written entirely between Mallorca, Menorca, Corfu, and Paxos, owes much to the inspiration offered by these islands.

Contents

Chapter 0

Heading For A New World

NOUR WAS born in Damascus, the city that was a living jewel, carved by millennia of culture. Her childhood memories were lost in the bustle of the old quarter, where the narrow, winding streets were permeated with the smell of fresh cedar and spices, and where craftsmen polished wooden and ivory boxes and fine ceramics at the entrances of the small shops. They also held sad memories of her early youth, her mother's death and the outbreak of war.

She had to abruptly move abroad at the age of fifteen. When the first bombs exploded, her father was one of the first in the city to decide to emigrate from Syria. Some of her uncles had been living in Hamburg for years, and they assured him that the northern German city would be a good place both for his children and for his career as a surgeon and researcher. So, they moved there. Her father's prestige as one of the most respected oncologists in the Middle East saved her from the harsh spiral of hate and destruction that soon engulfed her country.

Hamburg gradually shaped her adolescence and set her onto the path to a new life. Emotionally, it was not easy, but a strong bond with her two older brothers protected her from sadness and discouragement. Yet, the first years in that different and distant society were difficult, and she often felt marginalised. The language barrier, customs, and prejudices of many people forced her into introspection. This emotional loneliness made her stronger over time, and she put all her efforts into her studies to gain respect and acceptance. She ended up transforming difficulty into success. Heiress to her father's scientific streak, she was always interested in new technologies, spending hours and hours in her father's library on her computer, learning about artificial intelligence. This was a subject she found fascinating because it was always ahead of her imagination. Every time she imagined something that would transform the world, it would turn out to have already been proposed and on its way to becoming a reality. The vitality of that field led her to admire the great capacity of human intelligence. This passion soon led her to specialise in the study of emerging technologies. At the age of twenty-two, she graduated with top honours, and at twenty-eight, she was appointed professor at the Hamburg University of Technology. Since then, her reputation had grown steadily, and she had become an authority on research in the new fields of application of emerging technologies.

A beautiful, enigmatic, and warmly sensual woman, Nour possessed an unfathomable gaze. This gaze was a result of her dual scientific and humanist roots—cold, analytical, and precise as a scientist, yet enthusiastic, close, and sensitive as a humanist. Clearly, she had a knack for pure sciences as well as management.

She was seen as a particularly brilliant child in primary school in Damascus, where everyone considered her a prodigy, always representing the school in the youth competitions in mathematics and science. Later, in Germany, she always scored the highest in all areas of science, and was awarded a scholarship from start to finish by the university. But she was never an isolated scientist in an ivory tower. She always saw science as the most advanced arm of humanity to transform reality. At university, she specialised in exploring the imaginative functions of artificial brains and their organisational ability to develop new activities and open up new horizons for societies. She always had her sights set on driving development and discovery. She had, as her first tutor at the University of Hamburg had told her, an analytical mind in a body that exuded life and passion.

When she finished her studies, the first crisis of the twenty-first century reached the most indebted countries in Europe. Germany was able to weather it well. At that time, Nour founded a new knowledge company with the brightest colleagues from the university to implement artificial intelligence systems in business. It was a success, expanding rapidly. In the second decade of the century, her success continued, and she became an advisor to several industrial groups that wanted to accelerate the incorporation of emerging technologies. She also began to participate in many congresses and conferences on artificial intelligence. Her papers were coveted, and for the last five years she practically lived in airplanes, hopping from one continent to another in a frenzy. She became part of a select group of scientists driving the emergence of a new reality. At the same time, she discovered wonderful people and places that she wrote about in her logbook, hoping to visit them with greater calm and tranquillity.

The more she travelled, the more she became convinced of the infinite possibilities of the planet and its enormous wonders. She regretted that most people died without even knowing of their existence. She felt it was almost an affront to inhabit such a unique place and pass through it, as if, on tiptoe. She felt that the most important thing was to enable each person to discover their potential, develop their talent and explore what the world had to offer. Her interest in developing artificial intelligence systems, and specifically its implementation, was to facilitate new fields of expansion for humanity, bringing hitherto unknown capabilities to the surface. They could contribute to crucial breakthroughs. She sensed a promising future on the horizon and was determined to sail towards it with artificial intelligence to open up a fascinating new era.

With all the excitement of youth, she wanted to innovate and contribute to the transformation of the world.

This period of great activity was halted for a few months by the pandemic which immobilised everything. The world suddenly started shutting itself up as if in a shell, hibernating as snails or bears do. Everyone was seized by a deep fear of falling ill or dying, as if illness or death had not existed before and had suddenly entered the world on the wings of a new virus. The authorities advised isolation, as if the possibility of dying were a curse that had come upon them.

But death had never disappeared; everyone's desire to shut themselves away in false self-protection had frozen the collective life of the planet. Mass withdrawal undermined the basis of a global society built on the foundation of increasing contacts, eliminating distances, and minimising the space barriers. And just as a devastating earthquake causes even the most solid buildings to be swallowed up by the earth in a few seconds, entire sectors of the economy entered the black hole of bankruptcy and disappearance within a few months. Everyone wanted to resist, but many succumbed.

Under the lockdown, Nour spent her time in her apartment overlooking the Elbe, quite close to the harbour in Hamburg. Her thoughts turned to how to organise the world better, how artificial intelligence could serve the collective life in the future, overcoming the old-fashioned bureaucracies that had exposed its obsolescence and devising new projects that could be born under its impetus. 'This pandemic,' she reflected, 'has shown that we need to fundamentally transform the public sector to work like clockwork as the holder of regulatory power. The time has come to transform the substance of activity in all fields.' She was convinced that the exponential growth in the transmission of knowledge was enabling humans to become truly new intelligent beings.

During the long period of immobilisation, she explored new models of public organisation involving a leap in the management of collective challenges. She also researched on the new activities that could emerge by unlocking everyone's talents. 'The future,' Nour told herself, 'is leading us towards a world based on intelligence. The sooner we unleash every individual's creativity, the sooner we will reach the positive world that we need.'

'Artificial intelligence systems,' she thought, 'can organise many things in a new way. We cannot remain passive during the great crisis. Even if the breathing of the planet has been cut off for a moment, it has not finished with us! We have no choice but to grow in the face of difficulties! That must be the watchword of my generation! We must, by no means, be a fallen generation. On the contrary, we will take up the banner of ingenuity and creativity to enter a new era. We must be the generation of solutions, the one that faces the transformation of realities,' she said to herself with a certain emotion in her eyes. 'Yes, we must take a few steps back to leap towards greatness, as athletes do when they fly like gods with no other weapon than their impulse.'

'After the end of the lockdown,' she thought, 'a new space of freedom will open up. It may be short-lived because new waves of contagion may come, and the people will close in again. But it will be enough to reconnect with the most special places I've discovered along the way,' she thought.

'I will then meet those who can leverage artificial intelligence to drive forward projects that can transform the world. It will be valuable to use this window of freedom to visualise how much can be done in the future to establish a new possible world. This complex time must be the prelude to the beginning of a new era.'

Day by day, the idea took shape of using the period of discouragement and disorientation in all societies, to revisit the places that had most marked her in her travels around the world. She would contact people with whom she could further the implementation of new ideas and projects to open up new horizons of hope. 'Our only chance is to move forward and innovate,' she said decisively.

She knew that the initial stages following the end of lockdown would be tinged with unease and sadness. A globally paralysed world would leave a society deeply wounded and frightened, plunged into a previously unimaginable abyss. And even worse, full of fears and distant attitudes. 'To stop everything and get people to obey with a lower death toll, a lot of fear would have to be generated,' she thought. 'And then this fear, especially in affluent and aging societies where apprehension is strongest, would be hard to eradicate. For a while, nothing will keep up with last year's rapid pace, but we cannot give up and go back. The best I can do is to move forward, identifying the most innovative fields to incorporate new technologies in the world. We must show that there is a new north to head towards, even if there are stops along the way. We cannot lose momentum. We must begin to take action,' she said to herself.

And so she devised the idea of a unique journey, taking the pulse of the new possibilities that could open up in the world if we were to take a step forward with the help of artificial intelligence and act more creatively. She carefully planned the route to visualise the world of the future. Then she called Erika, her secretary, who was still working from home. She informed her of the new project to promote innovation in different fields, and instructed her on organising the logistics. It would be a complex and long trip, and she needed a good professional to make it possible to travel to each of the five continents in the way she had planned. They agreed that she would provide her with guidelines as the trip progressed. In some places, Nour would organise the transfers herself, but in others she would prefer Erika to take care of it.

Chapter 1

Towards Wadi Rum

Transforming the desert into a living world

ON THE day that Hamburg airport returned to normal, Nour set off on the journey she had planned. She would begin by returning to one of the most magical places she had discovered in the past, the desert of Wadi Rum. She packed up her entire flat, along with the documents that the Institute of the Future had shared about the congress for the new political architecture of the world. It was a promising congress scheduled to be held in Geneva in the middle of the year, but later got postponed until the following year because of the pandemic. Many thinkers were to participate in the congress to draw up the new rules governing the collective life of the planet in the future. She was called to participate with other experts regarding artificial intelligence contributing to better governance of the world.

Seeing everything in perfect order, she left, double-locked the door and set off for the airport. She was in high spirits. In those moments of collective immobilisation, she saw her journey as a mission—to envision the new world that might come by visiting places that inspired her. On her return, she would see the way to propel the ongoing changes. The new generation should be encouraged to be the driving force behind the great transformation.

The flight to Amman had been re-established after the great universal hiatus and it was now possible to travel from Amman to the great desert. The desert attracted her like a magnet. The flight had passed like a whisper, with the thrill of regaining her freedom and the excitement of starting a grand experience. She flew over the Mediterranean and the great deserts of Algeria, Libya, and Egypt, but at no time did the journey become monotonous. And as the plane soared, her thoughts swirled and gave her an intoxicating energy. 'How wonderful to be able to fly again,' she said to herself gathering the papers on which she had been fixing her thoughts when the pilot announced the start of the descent.

She landed in Amman and went through the entry formalities without any hassle. Like all newly-opened airports, the one in Amman was a shadow of what it had been before the collapse. She preferred not to think too much about it, so as not to get depressed, and soon reached the exit. There was no shortage of drivers offering their services. She chose the one that seemed the most cheerful, and in little more than three hours she reached her destination.

Everything was majestic in Wadi Rum! Its beauty was mesmerising as the vivid red sand combined with the rough, old, exhausted layer of earth of the small hills running unevenly for hundreds of miles. The breathtaking sunrise was etched in her mind, a pink-fingered aurora, as Homer defines it in the *Odyssey.* It was there where the sunrise drags a trail of pastel colours tinting the sky a pale pink, and soon the soft aurora turns to fire and the red areas take centre stage. That dawn has stayed with her as much as the deep silence that reigns during the day under the torrid sun. The combination of the deafening silence and the grandeur of the space had marked her. It connected her with the pristine nature.

She wanted to charge herself with the strength of the desert to start her long and diverse journey around the planet, to leave with energy in the face of the sadness of the moment. Some time ago, she had spent a night in one of the tents of the ecolodge set up by a very determined Bedouin couple, Mohad and Fahma, among the rock formations near the village of Rum. Nour was sure that nothing would have changed for them. Her intuition could not fail, and the car took her there skirting the coast of the Dead Sea.

She arrived just as the sun was beginning to set, tinting the vast expanse of red sand and small hills in beautiful shades of ochre, slowly turning to purple. She surprised Mohad and Fahma as they were preparing their frugal dinner for the day, some bread baked over a slow fire, a little goat's milk, some cheese, and a few almonds. This is what the land gave them and what they ate in small portions every night. Joy lit up everyone's faces.

'I have come to spend a few days with you, taking the outstretched hand you offered when I left a few years ago,' Nour said to them by way of greeting, and to address the surprise she saw on the couple's faces.

Fahma gave her a hug and Mohad a warm welcome, 'You know our heart is sincere. We told you when you left that nothing would make us happier than for you to return to us one day, and we thank Allah for making it a reality. Today is a great day for us, and we thank the great God for bringing you back and accompanying us again.'

And so began her second stay in Wadi Rum, a stay that would last for a few days marked by long forays into the infinite desert. Mohad left her one of his camels to explore that paradise. She had asked him how far it reached, and he had told her that he had never reached its limits, but that once, some wise foreigners, always very well informed, he said with a wry smile on his face, had told him that it was more than 800 kilometres. A little less than the vast desert of Persia or Arabia, he had been told, but more impressive because of the ruggedness of the old hills that mark it out for miles and miles. When she told him that she would love to explore it, he immediately offered her one of his camels.

She would set off in the morning, wrapped in veils and scarves from head to toe. This was the best way to survive the heat and the omnipotent power of the sun. The beginning of the march was always pleasant. You could breathe the smell of earth in the morning, when the humidity of the sand from the cold of the night evaporated with the first caresses of the sun. It was an unforgettable, powerful smell, which carried the strength of the solid earth.

On the third night, when she returned to the lodge after a day's journey around the small oases scattering the land in the north, she found that Mohad and Fahma had prepared a special welcome for her. Mohad had travelled to Rum that morning, and his cousin had given him one of the lambs slaughtered the previous night. Fahma had put it in a large clay jar and buried it in the sand, covering it with coals and roasting it for more than ten hours. It was now ready to be served and, after sprinkling it with honey and rosemary, eaten with the hands as the Bedouins do at sunset.

It was an incomparable dinner. The silence, the beauty of the colours in the sky, the seclusion of the sunburned hills, together with the flavours of honey and rosemary overlapping the slightly salty taste of the tender lamb melting between the fingers, created an unforgettable moment.

'You know?' Nour said as she sipped her mint tea,

'you have a jewel in your midst. The day someone knows how to organise tourism in the desert, it will be one of the most promising occupations of the new world. To be able to facilitate the discovery of silence and life amid immensity; the experience of breathing in the smell of dry earth every morning; of tasting this exquisite lamb cooked in harmony with nature, roasted within it—is destined to be a form of new wealth if done intelligently.'

Fahma nodded with a look of hope but also disbelief. She could hardly imagine how this could be possible over hundreds of kilometres with hardly any roads and no planned infrastructure.

'What you say,' Mohad replied, 'is impossible. If it is not well organised, it will spoil what little we have of wonder, and if it is well organised, it will require a prodigious mind. Hundreds of roads would have to be opened, but concealed to not affect the immensity of this geography. It would need thousands of small houses distanced by miles to maintain the silence of the visitors' unique experience. So many other things would have to be thought of, so many details, to skilfully combine activity and preservation, that it is an undertaking to even imagine it.'

'True,' said Nour, 'you and I can only imagine. But what is certain is that the desert is a virgin field; the pioneers and visionaries who decide to do it, if they plan it well, will open up a horizon of wealth for this region which is now considered a wasteland. Besides, transportation in the future may be by drones that do not require roads or land infrastructure.'

'When the insecurities cease and we enter a more positive world, then, and only then, perhaps it will be possible,' Mohad responded with a halo of sadness.

'Hopefully one day it will come true,' Nour replied calmly. 'Throughout history, the Arab world has had moments of marvellous splendour. It has shown supreme skills in both art and science. Who does not recognise its contribution to mathematics and sciences, such as astronomy or physics that were developed later?

'Who does not rank the ancient cities of Babylon, Nineveh, or Sidon among the most beautiful cities of mankind? That ability to think and act on a large scale is precisely what is needed now. In a world where we must think of new activities, this is the virgin ground that we must till with intelligence.'

Mohad nodded and, in a somewhat resigned tone, told her, 'It would be wonderful if your generation, people who have seen their lives and hopes shattered by the pandemic, could now rise up with their resilience and use what they have learned in architecture, organisation, and logistics, to be the pioneers of this transformation. What an accomplishment it would be if they could make of the desert a new sea of spiritual beauty for millions of people who would come here to witness the unique splendour that so many people die without knowing of.'

Her eyes watered and, taking his hand in hers, Nour replied with great enthusiasm, 'I hope we can see it! It's about doing extremely beautiful work at an almost infinite scale. Here in Jordan, there is Wadi Rum, but neighbouring Iran has an even greater desert, as do Saudi Arabia and Egypt. There are huge areas where silence reigns amid a virgin and austere but enormously powerful nature. In the past, Arabs knew how to create the Alhambra and the most harmonious gardens. Today, the challenge lies in knowing how to use the immensity of the deserts to create unique experiences for people. In a world where energies are transforming and the richness of black gold is coming to an end, we have to find the new gold to replace it. This also means accepting the hand of the future. It needs to open a great field for architecture and hospitality that gives initiative to millions of people. It has to replace the verticality of oil power by the horizontality of an activity sustained by thousands of entrepreneurs. This challenge can be supported by artificial intelligence, which would create virtual assistants working seamlessly and organising the activities. It can be met with success!'

Nour then recalled the conversation she had a year ago with the Egyptian Minister of Tourism, Anat Said, during their visit to the Valley of the Kings. The Minister, a well-educated person who had worked for years in the major international financial institutions in Washington, was receptive to new and fresh ideas. Following a lecture Nour had given in Cairo on the applications of artificial intelligence in the cultural field, the Minister had invited her to visit the treasures hidden in the ancient beautiful tombs. The beauty of the inner paradises of the great tombs had impressed her. 'No one should leave this world without having walked through the interior of the tomb of Ramses IX or the tomb of Amenhotep II, and without being enraptured by the sarcophagus of the young Tutankhamun. The great legacy of humanity should be a living part of everyone's life,' she thought at the time.

In the evening, as they talked about the future on the terrace of the Winter Palace Hotel in Luxor, she began to fit the pieces together in organising a new tourism dynamic linking the discovery of the culture of the past with the unique experience of immersing oneself in the grandeur of the desert. The Minister was keen to learn more about knowledge technologies and its evolution in the first world. Nour, for her part, was focused on utilising artificial intelligence to open up a future for millions of people.

'You have it in your hands to bring greatness back to your country,' Nour said to Anat. 'In history, there have always been people who blaze trails. From the great explorers and inventors to the great artists, it is the visionaries who leave their mark and widen horizons. You hold in your hands two great riches—the unrepeatable millenary culture and the incomparable grandeur of the desert. You lack only a third element, an organised way to offer all this to millions of people in the world without spoiling it, thereby empowering your compatriots to develop small stays as an oasis of tranquillity. This is your challenge—to match architecture, infrastructure, and a culture of hospitality. However, it is less difficult than reaching the moon, or sailing the depths of the oceans, though we have done both.

'So if we've done both, why can't you take on this one?' she encouraged Anat as she stared into her eyes, searching for the complicity of two women passionate about the future.

The difference was that Nour travelled very fast with her mind, while Anat felt the weight of the difficulty of transforming realities. Anat then took Nour by the hand, and said with sympathy,

'It would be so beautiful if we could do it. It would give life and open the minds of millions of people. But I could only go down this path if I was certain that we would not spoil anything. First, we must develop a model that allows millions of people to gently discover the grandeur that history and nature have bequeathed to us. Let's think about it. I like the idea of creating artificial intelligence systems leading to smart integral development of these great spaces. By combining data on the configuration of the desert, the distances between lodges to ensure solitude and security, calculating the ideal layout of mobility circuits by air through a new generation of safe drones, and many other variables, you can build a new sustainable development model that seduces humanity and opens up the wealth of the desert to the people.'

That had been the first time she had thought about it and now, discussing this with Mohad, she realised how carefully she had kept it in her mind. She wondered why, maybe it was her way of giving something back to her home culture. Bringing the magical soul of the Arab world back into the light! Subconsciously, she felt that the wonder of the deserts of the Middle East and its ancient cultures deserved a better fate in the world of the future.

'Nour, you always whet our appetite for something big,' Fahma said fondly, as she offered her the baklava she had carefully prepared in the afternoon.

'And I am always grateful for your generosity and connection to the grandeur of the desert. Thank you for giving me back the energy,' she replied with a small crack of emotion in her voice.

'Yes,' Mohad interjected, 'what you've told us gives me a lot to think about. No doubt you are leaving behind a seed that I will spread, and when you return, I will hopefully be able to tell you that your ideas have taken root.'

The conversation had run long, while they carefully sketched the innovative project that could give value to the desert, putting the country back on track. Now the time had come to say goodbye, and they marched towards their tents, hugging each other and admiring a sky dotted with millions of stars. Once inside the tent, Nour blew out the candles and went to bed. Soon she fell into a deep sleep, and dreamed that she was part of a great debate on the future of the world in the summit called to reorganise humanity as a whole to move towards a new and higher stage. The conference was about to start, and in her dreams, she entered the room where those who could build the foundations of the new common home were meeting.

Chapter 2

Towards The World Of One Humanity

NOUR DREAMT being invited to the great assembly laying the foundations of the world's new political architecture. In her dreams, she entered the most beautiful room in the headquarters of the United Nations, whose dome, a pictorial work by Miquel Barceló, crowns the Chamber of Human Rights and the Alliance of Civilisation like the bottom of an inverted sea. There, the UN Secretary-General had summoned people who could significantly contribute to reorganising the world and overcoming the global economic and social catastrophe that followed the pandemic.

The depth of the crisis had opened the door to rethink the future of humanity. And that's where Nour came in—amazed and excited to listen to the great debate lighting up the new world. The man whom everyone expected as capable of doing everything, took the rostrum first, and he began to deliver a speech that would awaken everyone's ambitions and point out the possible path to follow.

'Today,' he said, 'we irrefutably feel that we are all equally fragile on this planet. The pandemic has crossed all borders and reminded us of the value of humanity. We have seen that all of us—Europeans, Asians, Africans, Americans—have been overwhelmed by a pandemic that has had no regard for borders or human differences, only for each body's capacity to resist. The condition of being human has been the only thing that mattered to the disease, and yet, this is what has united all researchers in the search for a solution.

'Today, we have begun to neutralise it, but we must take it as a warning and start moving towards a new goal before a greater evil leads us to irreparable disaster. The pandemic has spread like a piercing silence and has quickly frozen the life of the planet in its tracks. And I want to say what many on all five continents feel—we have learned that we cannot open the door to any major disaster without paying a very high price in levels of well-being. And the major disaster threatening us is the risk of a war which, because of its nuclear, chemical, or biological component, would be infinitely worse than this pandemic.

'The pandemic has crippled us and sent millions of people into poverty in the blink of an eye, despite nations' production capacities, technological advances, and channels of cooperation. How can then a new-generation war be feasible while rendering everything inoperative?

The first lesson we must learn from this pandemic is that we must end the diabolic dream of those who wish to trigger wars and massive destruction.

'How can some people think that after launching not just one virus but a combination of viruses, or after detonating their atomic bombs, they will be able to maintain civilisation as we know it today? If they survive, they will experience atrocious deaths due to permanent contamination. Undoubtedly, those surviving the hecatomb would immediately return to the caves. Everyone, absolutely everyone, would lose in this scenario.

'Today, we have seen our collective life get disorganised at such great speed that we are approaching the abyss of poverty, famine, sanitary collapse, and despair within a few months. Imagine what would have become of our lives if this virus had invaded not in one wave of contagion, but in multiple waves and variants after bacteriological bombings. This virus shows that nuclear, bacteriological, or chemical weapons are not really usable, as using them would lead to the defeat of all. Or, does the potential winner believe that they could continue to produce and consume as before even in the present modernity? No, if they survive, they will be condemned to live in the caves again. They will suffer terrible illnesses because healthcare will collapse and treatments will disappear. The survivors will live in agony and constant suffering. They will live an atrocious life in an atrocious world.

'And, what is next for us today? Today, we can move towards the most promising moment in our history as humanity. We have now made it possible to talk to each other in real time across distant continents. We have ensured that a great pandemic, which has always resulted in years of suffering and chilling death tolls, has been stopped in a short time and with a very low percentage of deaths in a world of 8 billion people. In our long evolution, we have overcome great scourges, some of them as terrible as slavery and wars. And today, we see a world full of life. Let us not destroy our hope. Let us not stifle our flourishing.

'What kind of world is on the horizon? The world of intelligent humanity. The world of mankind as a work force, as an instrument to be used by fellows, is coming to an end. The time has come to unlock the talents of all of us who make up humanity. And, we can neither betray nor let this great moment slip away. We are close to the world of creativity, where everything we can imagine can be transformed into reality. We cannot remain at its doors and close them abruptly because of the ego of some or the miscalculation of others!

'And, why might these doors be closed? Because we are determined to continue with the same dynamic of separating people into groups, nations, cultures, and civilisations as we did before the pandemic. There are only two paths left for us. We can either move towards the future, providing a stable framework for all humanity and making every human being an essential part of our progress, relying on each individual's creative capacity, the new world of "One Humanity". Alternatively, we can continue to play with fire, leading to the end of the world by keeping it fragmented in groups and nations.

'Unfortunately, the focus is still on group traits, the importance of this or that country, and every other thing that differentiates and separates us. It is true that difference exists just as biodiversity exists in nature. But, difference is a value and a richness, not a synonym for the inability to understand each other or hate each other. The deep-seated drive to dominate and destroy prevails in this second option.

'And does this mean that the nations and the organisation over which I preside, with more than 190 nations represented here, are a mistake, a failed project? No, a hundred times no! We have been able to push the collective ship forward. We have developed important collective rules, such as the Universal Declaration of Human Rights, and we have set global goals and commitments so that progress can be shared, such as the Sustainable Development Goals and the 2030 Agenda. And because of this global political organisation, we can devise a more sophisticated structure. I would like to say to the honourable national representatives, that you represent a good way of organising and structuring societies, but we cannot stop here because the ground has been prepared to move on to the next one. You have a mission to accomplish—to be the channels carrying us to the new organisational system of humanity.

'Water does not flow into the sea in a disorderly way; nature channels it through rivers. Similarly, you represent the most perfect way in which we have organised ourselves to reach the common sea, our ultimate structural goal, the "One Humanity" world. You are the channels through which diverse groupings of people can converge towards a single space, the sea of humanity in common.

'We have evolved through larger and larger organised political spaces. We jumped from our tiny family group to the tribe, from the tribe to the village, from village to region, from region to small kingdoms, then to nations and, finally, to large, federated spaces. Today, destiny demands us to take a step further and anchor a new world order on a global scale. It needs a new way of organising ourselves that guarantees general stability and unblocks everyone's talent everywhere.

'I would like to announce that we are gathered here to lay the foundations for the new world of "One Humanity", and we must be ready to hear from those who can contribute to making this noble ambition a reality. We are a generation with the capacity to act. Not only can we dream and imagine more than any previous generation, but we can also transform dreams and ideas into reality.

That is why, we should not stop.

'Let us listen to all who can enlighten us on how to achieve this; let us step towards this profound transformation of our world. We need a guiding North to eliminate the drift towards confrontation, and a conviction must impel us to build a world where innovation holds the key and helps foster freedom everywhere.'

And then, at the end of the speech, the audience applauded thunderously. Enthusiasm filled the room and the man took his seat to listen to the first of the speakers.

Chapter 3

To Socotra

The islands, new jewels of globality

AFTER DAWN, Nour said an early goodbye to Mohad and Fahma and left for Aqaba. From there, she took a boat towards Oman and sailed for more than five days down the Red Sea until she reached the Yemeni island of Socotra.

She had been there a few years ago; the Sultan had invited her to talk about artificial intelligence. Qaboos bin Said Al Said was an extremely cultured Sultan, devoted to making Muscat the cultural capital of the Arabian Peninsula during his fifty years of rule. In the last years of his life, he had been passionate about artificial intelligence, and all of Nour's books featured prominently in his library. She often corresponded with him to keep him abreast of developments and to organise interesting lectures. Since then, the royal family's investments in companies dedicated to artificial intelligence had multiplied. In the first year, she had been told so much about Socotra, its beauty and magic shrouded in mist, that she had decided to stop there for a day before returning home. The island enchanted her, and she decided that one day she would explore it further. Now that the world had almost come to a standstill, she could make her wish come true.

The passage through the Red Sea was of unparalleled beauty. The incomparable journey sometimes brought them close to the coasts of Saudi Arabia and Yemen and other times those of Egypt, Eritrea, and Somalia. Time seemed suspended in the immense deserts stretching for miles and miles, bathed by crystal clear waters, tinged pale blue and turquoise green by the corals near the shores. It was the purity of the ocean in its absolute state, and Nour enjoyed its beauty amidst the fiery sun and the lapping of serene waters. Abdalah, the sailor, fixed the rudder with a rope and leaned against the left angle of the stern to get the maximum shade cast by the cabin tent, while telling stories about the ports where they spent the night.

He recounted many of Alexander the Great's exploits in those lands. And, at dusk, it was a privilege to stop at the small ports, descend and be instantly surrounded by Nubian or Bedouin children, with their piercing gaze and infinite curiosity. This bustle was a blessing after hours and hours of leisurely sailing alone. They ate little during the day, only the supplies of almonds and nuts they had on-board. In the evenings, they always roasted some fish caught during the voyage.

After descending the Red Sea, they turned at the

cape of Guardafui and saw Socotra in the distance. The tiny island defying the immensity of the ocean seemed a wonder to Nour. As they approached, she saw the small hotel where she had stayed the first time, on the hill next to the lighthouse. She disembarked and soon found that everything was still the same. Time had left no trace of change on the island that was almost independent from the world. 'Islands really are the best places to take refuge from pandemics or great collective disasters,' thought Nour, 'and they are often sublime places as well.' She recalled that Plato had built an ideal society despising everything but knowledge and virtue on the great island of Atlantis.

After docking, she jumped onto the dock and walked quietly towards the hotel. Raschid, the owner's son, remembered her though it had been a few years since her brief stay.

'Ms Aswad, I can't tell you how glad I am to have you back. My mother will be very happy to see you again,' he said greeting her before running to his mother's room. They gave Nour the largest room, the one that faced the sea and from which you could see the early morning sunrise—big, red, powerful, slow—over the ocean!

'You'll be fine here,' Hayfa, the landlady, told her. 'No one will disturb you. Only Naguib, the lighthouse keeper, sleeps on this floor at the other end. He is a quiet man and comes here only on Saturday afternoons to rest because he has to sleep in the lighthouse on the other days. He has a very different life, but he is a very nice old man.'

'I'd love to meet him if it's alright with him,' Nour said.

'I'm sure he will appreciate that. He hasn't seen anyone new in a while as the pandemic hasn't brought any ships these past few months. I'll suggest you have dinner together this Saturday,' Hayfa concluded.

Nour settled comfortably in her room and began drafting her report on the future application of artificial intelligence in island development. She had always been passionate about islands, seeing them as isolated diamonds in globalisation. She believed that they would be the most desirable territories on the planet in the future. She understood that the lack of connectivity in the past had left them on the margins of the evolution of the world. Traditionally, it had always been more difficult to get things and information to the islands than to the mainland, which had deepened their isolation. On the other hand, the mobility of people was always limited. In the economy, they were always more marginalised because everything had higher costs and competitiveness suffered. Things had begun to change with the development of modern shipping and aviation revolution. But it was only with the advent of instant communication and development of the service industry that the islands were beginning to climb the world's ladder. With newer technologies, the sea was now gaining new value as a source of energy. Water could be desalinated, thereby flourishing the local agriculture. The world was beginning to know no bounds for the islands, and it was time to ponder over their growth for they were emerging as precious but fragile places! Their place in the world would be irreplaceable if they could combine modernity and uniqueness.

Before the pandemic, several American islands had teamed up to organise a major conference on discussing their future. She had been chosen as the keynote speaker on artificial intelligence systems' contribution to their development. The pandemic had postponed the meeting, giving her more time to reflect on a subject she found promising. 'There are clear chapters,' she thought, 'for example, the ability to tackle fires. With aerial equipment and new technologies, fires should become a thing of the past on the islands. The sea offers an unparalleled insurance when aircraft and drones can collect water in abundance, giving them a unique comparative advantage. Even the worst-case scenario of night fires could be neutralised as drones can operate in the dark. The challenge is to convince the authorities to change their registry and immediately equip themselves with large aerial fleets. Each fire lasts hours or days, but it takes thirty years for nature to recover! Every minute gained is essential, and only by utilising aerial equipment could the islands tackle forest fires at the slightest hint of smoke. They have a great advantage over other territories as they are surrounded by water, but this advantage will only make a difference if the leaders equip themselves with the air assets they need.'

She had opened several chapters to emphasise at the congress and, in all of them, she insisted on innovation to strengthen the islands' future. 'We are in a world that will see tourism grow exponentially, and if they know how to attract the highest quality flows, the islands can be big winners,' she thought. 'Now that we have entered a waiting period due to the pandemic, it is time to think how the islands will absorb this growth. They must set their sights on being the jewels, the most sophisticated territories welcoming tourist flows. And the issue is so complex that a good scenario simulation with algorithms is needed. To guide the decision-makers, we must combine all the data—new activities required to become wonderful host territories, existing strengths and weaknesses, and costs and difficulties of the measures to be adopted. A study on the cost of poor choices would be very useful. With the standstill imposed by the pandemic, the time is right to redirect its growth towards the path of quality,' she reckoned.

Thus, she worked for several days to articulate various models of harmonious future development for small- and medium-sized islands. Since tourism is a horizontal industry involving the participation of many actors, it was essential to devise coordinated plans between them. Coordination meant thinking about territorial planning, infrastructures, transport connections, architecture of houses and hotels, the culture on offer, and so on and so forth. To coordinate everything, in-depth knowledge is essential. To make the point, she would present the image of the palm tree to the audience—a large central trunk and a multitude of large, strong leaves, all with a life of their own, symmetrical but independent. The central trunk represented the determination to turn the islands into jewels of world tourism. This trunk was to give life to the branches which, being symmetrical but independent, were born with an overall harmony. The branches had a range of themes like 'clean waters', 'architecture that exudes art', 'new epicentres of cultural initiatives', etc. 'These spaces deserve a development that aims at quality in new growth. It is complex, but possible,' she said to herself, enthusiastically writing the notes to organise her proposal.

She had been working all week; the serenity of Socotra helped her in outlining every idea of her lecture in detail. She was glad to have been able to take refuge there for a few days. The week flew by so quickly that the early dinner on Saturday, arranged for her by Hayfa with the lighthouse keeper, came almost as a surprise.

They had set up a small round table on the hotel's tiny terrace facing the ocean, under the shade of two large mimosa trees, which made it even more pleasant at sunset. Hayfa made the introductions and soon Naguib and Nour began to hit it off. The sturdy man with the long white beard and bright, toasted almond-coloured eyes, with hard, rough skin, seemed to be timeless. It was hard to tell whether he was sixty, seventy or eighty years old. He had entered a quiet equilibrium in his life and defied the passage of time with overwhelming dignity.

'Hayfa told me that this is your second time in Socotra,' he said, starting the conversation.

'Yes, I was here a few years ago, but only for one day. I was fascinated by the island and always dreamed of returning. Now, with everything on hold because of the pandemic, I've been able to find the time to do it. It's an enchanting island!'

'True,' he said, 'it is impressive how it emerges in solitude in the middle of the ocean. And yet you don't feel forgotten. The sea may seem monotonous, but it's like a never-ending mantra. There seems to be no diversity in it, but one can spend the whole day gazing at it without getting tired. I, who stare at infinity all day long, wonder how this is possible! I have spent the last fifty years watching the horizon for any ship that might have difficulties in this little-travelled but dangerous space because of the mists nearby, and I have never had a long day, nor have I thought of changing my job. I have always considered myself a privileged man. I think I will die looking at the sea; death will approach with the softness of the incoming sunset, closing the day without abruptness, with the lazy arrival of the night.'

'You are very lucky indeed,' said Nour, 'the islands are the magic points in the union of man with the land and the sea. But today, we have entered a new epoch in which the sea acquires a new value, inviting new perspectives for the islands. You have been able to experience it like no one else in the tranquillity of Socotra, and I intend to study and arrange it so that the whole world can enjoy it,' she said.

'Oh, please don't address me formally,' he protested with a smile. 'I am old and you are young, but we are kindred spirits, and the spirit is what matters. Let us speak like friends. I am glad that you have understood the greatness of the islands and that you can spread their value. And above all, I am glad that you are working to reconcile fragility and development. It says a lot about your sensitivity and subtlety.' After a brief silence, he added, 'Do you know what the most beautiful thing about Socotra is?'

'No,' she replied, inviting him to continue.

'The caves that extend into the sea. When you dive into them and explore underwater, you discover a blue that covers everything. Then, at the bottom, you find the most luxuriant corals, where an extraordinary variety of fish nest. Nature could not have created anything more sublime. It is beauty in its purest state, unparalleled! I've spent so many days immersing myself in it that I assure you, you'll discover something unforgettable if you do so before leaving.' And then, he took out a sheet of paper with a map of Socotra and pointed to the cave. 'It is the blue cave par excellence, a marvellous place for its light and depths, because, as I was telling you, in the concave spaces the land lets the sea penetrate into its depths, and you find the most unsurpassed corners of the islands.

Thanks to this special intersection of sea and land, every island becomes incomparable!'

Nour understood that this tranquillity had allowed the man to observe nature in detail and that nature, when experienced up close, was even more prodigious. During that dinner, she learned a lot about the solitary struggle of the islands to exist.

The man had witnessed the fury of the waves and typhoons on many occasions, and his account ultimately depicted the island as a unit of heroic resistance to the force of the ocean.

'The most amazing thing about life on the island,' he told her at the end of the night, 'is that its insertion into the ocean so enraptures its inhabitants that it makes them quite unique. Instead of uniting the locals, the island turns them into circumspect beings. And, I think, it's because it brings people so close to the sea that one tends not to want to expend energy on other things,' he said, stroking his beard, looking for support for his words.

Nour pondered, a humanity eager to rediscover nature and possessing the technology to be united at a distance could turn the islands into one of the most precious places in the world. 'It is important that my generation moves forward in strengthening the islands' uniqueness which gives it a new global role,' she thought. The islands can be one of the best places to explore new possibilities—a vast field of holistic development models working with artificial intelligence systems to transform them into intelligent territories. 'Yes,' she said to herself, 'the field is open for my generation to contribute significantly.'

Before dinner ended, Nour and Naguib exchanged some anecdotes. His talked about the tension between Yemen and its neighbours over control of the island. Hers were about the surprising twists and turns she had experienced while experimenting with artificial intelligence. And as they said their goodbyes, he advised, 'Highlight the potential of the islands, but maintain their character as solitary and fascinating territories!'

The next afternoon, Nour and Raschid went down the small mountain following the route opposite the harbour, overlooking the virgin sea. From there, they jumped into the water to reach the blue cave that Naguib had drawn on the map the night before. They swam along the shore for some time and, just as they were beginning to feel tired, they saw the entrance between two large rocks anchored in the sea. They dove in, entering a unique experience. Never before had Nour seen such bright blue water and so much life at the foot of the corals. There were starfish of all sizes and brightly coloured fish. It was a paradise of beauty. 'In such an extraordinary world,' she thought, 'my generation must make the intelligent development of the islands an essential part of its contribution.'

Nour and Raschid dove deeper and discovered many interior passages in that seemingly endless cave. They both lost track of time, and when they came out, they saw that the sun was already setting. They swam fast so that the night would not catch up with them in the water, and arrived nearly exhausted at the rock from where they had jumped into the sea. They took a few minutes to regain strength and, under moonlight, climbed the path that led to the hotel. Nour packed her suitcase for an early departure the next day and went to bed exhausted. Within a few minutes, she was sleeping soundly; sleep took her back to the great assembly called to lay the foundations of the new political architecture of the world.

Chapter 4

The Hour Of The Philosopher

IN HER dream, the 'wise' man spoke. He was so called because he was the most renowned philosopher on the planet. His thoughts had taken on everything—from the most metaphysical questions to questions concerning the moral codes humanity could share before its departure into the cosmos. He had also reflected on what values could unite civilisations across the world when the technological era had eliminated the small, unique cultural universes, and had precipitated the humanity into a common dynamic.

He began his speech by calling for a moral code uniting everyone in a possible harmony. 'It is an honour for me to take the floor after the Secretary-General of the United Nations,' he said, looking soberly at the audience, 'in whom you have placed your hopes to seal the new covenant on which to build the trust of humanity, and to begin the march into the future on a secure and inclusive basis. I deeply respect him and am grateful that he has convened such a diverse assembly to listen to those who look at the future from a different angle of knowledge to move towards such a noble goal.'

He spoke in a leisurely, understated tone, as if to announce that his exposition would be more solemn than those to follow, without making his words any less important in forming a new consciousness.

'I am here today to try to channel man's deepest yearnings, to triumph and dominate, under a new code of conduct that uses his strength to progress and avoids the misfortune of shock and destruction which he carries within. These have been two great motors giving us both sublime moments and tremendous tragedies. Today, they must be combined with the two great emerging forces of our time, the capacity for production, which opens the doors of everything to everyone; and the techno-sciences that have come to transform our lives. The techno-sciences must align with our destiny and interests so that they may always be our loyal companion and not a new indomitable problem of the future. At this crossroads, the best thing is to establish a complete moral code of humanity, a code facilitating collective coexistence in a constantly evolving world, a code composed of basic but broad norms, free from religions and ideologies. The code should distinguish this humanity and accredit it as the bearer of good, one whose fundamental pillar may well be harmony. Making harmony the keystone of humanity's actions will lead to peace and tolerance. The willingness to understand and interact positively will nourish the lives of all.

'In the last century, at the end of the Second World War, we took a great step forward by adopting the Universal Declaration of Human Rights, a fundamental charter to guide dialogue between States and to anchor universal standards of dignity for all human beings. Today, we must go even further by adopting a shared code of conduct as a solid anchor—one that enables individuals to participate autonomously, without repressive limits.

'Since the origins of our species, the gods have fixed the conduct of men and women in the various civilisations. A few millennia ago, we had many gods in the dominant civilisations, some of them as inspiring to human destiny as the gods of the Egyptian universe or of Greek Olympus. They embodied the deep forces that animate our souls and helped us name our fears and hopes. With the evolution of civilisations, monotheistic religions appeared, shaping and structuring the major cultures for centuries. Today, with humanity leaping into space, we will be scattered across very distant galaxies in a few centuries. What a great achievement it would be if mankind could leave Earth having succeeded in establishing a way to organise itself globally. What a great achievement it would be if, after centuries of work, wars, and suffering, we were able to organise a positive interrelationship between all humans, just as nature has created a great cycle in the world, where millions of different species coexist in balance. In nature, all beings live and die freely, without a capacity for total destruction.

Nature has organised the life cycle of millions of beings in different states, whether they are plants or animals; whether they move on the ground, in the sea, or the air; whether they live for a few hours or hundreds of years. Similarly, we should at least be able to organise the interweaving of life in our species,' he said, pointing out how small our task was compared with the great work of nature.

'Our first goal should not be impossible, to organise ourselves to unleash each other's talents! From there, we must focus on articulating the relationship between everyone, finding ways to interact so that their capacities align, as the *input* of multiple collective chains that nourish each other without clashing or exclusion. If we achieve this, we will have laid the foundation for man and woman to go out into space as a civilisation of harmony that its own sustainable development model. The Earth will have lent us two hundred thousand years to achieve this, but today we are closer than ever before. We will have taken over from the gods entering our middle age, the age when we take our destiny into our own hands.'

The faces in the audience became grave. The weight and significance of his words struck a deep chord with all the delegates who recognised within themselves the great moral authority of the thinker.

'Our main challenge,' he continued, 'is to know how to organise ourselves as a single humanity and raise a harmoniously structured civilisation. We live on a planet where we have set ourselves up as the sole dominant species. It could not have been like that. We could live in a world where we had to confront other beings and focus on ensuring our survival, but no; there is no dominant species other than us. Today, our evolution has led us to be a species threatened only by its own capacity for destruction. Just having to care for ourselves is a great gift of destiny that we cannot squander because of the short-sightedness of those who wish to be the strongest humans, when what we truly need is to be the strongest entities in the universe! Our main challenge is with ourselves—not understanding how great we can be; our success lies in knowing how to organise ourselves to deploy all our positive capacity. And to take this knowledge to the cosmos if we succeed. Our task is great; let's not fail!

'Let us begin by consolidating a code of conduct that guides each individual towards a collective action in harmony. That is the great legacy that we must take to the cosmos. We are first and foremost spiritual beings, and the new era that we must now initiate must banish force, the central identity of primates. Instead it must be based on the capacity for understanding, the central element of intelligence. We have learned to survive and tame adverse forces. We are now moving towards taking our destiny into our own hands without gods. This means creating our mental universe, the overall code of conduct as humans.

'Great men and women have been marking our stages

with new thoughts and discoveries. With the emergence of Greek culture, we began the path of philosophy, moving autonomously within the implacable variant that is time. Chronos is certainly our limit that forces us to pass the baton to each other. Time exceeds the life of any individual, and we need to ensure that no relay jeopardises the progress that has been made. Hence, we must set the moral course that will guide the future of humanity, strengthen coexistence and prevent anything from blocking its constant evolution and yearning for all that is new. This should be our basis to flourish as a common civilisation in the diversity of the cosmos. The time has come to act, for the pandemic has reminded us that we are all the same—human.

'We are, then, facing one of those moments that produce vertigo. Many are concerned about leaving a better planet for their children. This is undoubtedly a worthy and honourable concern, but I would like to add that it is even more important to know what kind of children we will leave on the planet to ensure harmonious succession of generations. This is our greatest responsibility today—to guide the new generations towards a new moral horizon in search of human harmony achieved by our own thinking and efforts.

'Will we be able to create our own code of conduct based solely on the value of what is human, not on the dictates of gods, and sail the cosmos in the near future with a model of collective life? When we meet other species in the universe, will we shine as beings of a harmoniously articulated civilisation that has succeeded in making its home planet a place of mature coexistence? The time has come to grow, driven by what unites us, and to draw up the rules that will help us flourish and avoid destruction. I feel very honoured to place thought as a fundamental pillar of the construction of the new world based on its two children, values and principles, to start the new journey well equipped. The task has already begun. The Secretary-General has asked me to organise the work necessary to progress in this endeavour. Surely, the world of the humanity has been set in motion, and the mechanical framework to lay the solid foundations for the planet's vitality has begun to take shape. We need a planet with a soul, a planet that thanks man for its existence.

'With intelligence and healthy ambition, we will be able to promote a new political architecture that will close the door to destruction and open the floodgates to creativity. I pledge to work on this and to create a new code of values for humanity which, based on the Universal Declaration of Human Rights, will guarantee global coexistence and enable us to deploy our talents. It is in displaying collective artistry, delegates, that we will distinguish ourselves as a superior species.'

Picking up the papers of his speech, he left the gravity and ambition of his words floating in the audience.

Chapter 5

To Bombay

The challenge of urban planning and quality of life

IT WAS early morning when Nour took the flight from Socotra airport to Addis Ababa. At dawn, the island was wrapped in dense fog which misled sailors and caused many shipwrecks, but created a world of its own. Shortly after taking off in an old aircraft that connected the island with the big airport of the Ethiopian capital, the blue sky appeared, clean and infinite. Below, the white dot was seen as a cloud of cotton, growing smaller and smaller in the vast Indian Ocean. She soon arrived in Addis Ababa, where she was to connect at the airport with the direct flight to Bombay. The transfer went smoothly, and she was soon on board a modern Dreamliner, which would bring her to another continent in a few hours. She relaxed in the planes, and found human victory over space impressive, having succeeded in bringing the whole world within reach. 'What a marvellous revolution we've accomplished by taking off to the sky,' she always thought when the aircraft, under the compact noise of the engines, lifted its nose and began to fly through the sky. This time the plane did so very quietly, for the Dreamliner was the most quiet and environment-friendly of the existing planes. Nour thought about how far aviation was advancing to become increasingly sustainable.

She was passionate about that feeling of power and superiority of science, which she experienced on board an aeroplane.

Now she was on her way to one of the cities that overwhelmed and surprised her the most, Bombay. In her profession, Nour collaborated with a lot of Indian researchers. Certain circles in the country were a hotbed for new technology projects due to its long tradition of training mathematicians and engineers that provided an exceptional breeding ground. Though India was a country of striking dichotomy, there was an undercurrent of energy that united all its inhabitants and made the country special, as if it were a universe of its own in the global world.

She kept in touch with Hari Rahiv, with whom she discussed many of the new projects she was commissioned to do. The dialogue was always convoluted but useful. She would make strong progress initially, only to get entangled in small problems, but it gave her a different perspective. Once in the country, she would immerse herself in ordinary life, where bustle and chaos, wrapped in an innate confidence in surviving any setback, always impressed her. Her trips to India had always left a mark on her, right from the first time she landed in New Delhi, when her taxi dodged dozens of fearless tuk-tuks. Everything was a chaos that miraculously never exploded. Nowhere else could she see elephants, cars and motorbikes loaded with four people coexisting on urban roads without it all ending in tragedy. Sheltered by its greatness and legendary history, and embracing modernity in its own style, that country was another world.

Hari had gone to meet her at the airport. He was excited to share with Nour one of the assignments the government had just given him—to think of new urban planning models to harmoniously articulate the growth of medium-sized cities and small towns. The challenge was great, as great as the country. Overwhelmed by population growth and lack of order and harmony, the government had pinned its hopes on artificial intelligence. It believed that by cross-referencing data on the tastes and habits of the population, their mobility needs, land ownership, and the evolution of activities, it could come up with new settlement models that would combine harmony and social acceptance.

'I'm so glad you came,' he said as he received her. 'We have so much to do together!'

'Yes,' she said, 'but first take me to eat a good curry in one of those crowded places in the centre because I'm dying for a brush with life. I've had too many days of total calm, and now I need the uncontrolled bustle of Bombay!'

They crossed the Bandra-Worli Sea Link Bridge, which leads to the city and presents its best buildings before giving way to a centre full of chaos, misery, and life. The contrast between an absurd degree of modernity and huge pockets of poverty, coexisting without despising each other, is one of the most revealing features of Bombay. The character of a maritime city further lends the city its unique dynamism.

Hari chose one of the most popular places in the centre of the town for a nice spicy curry with mashed lentils and the melted cheese-stuffed naan bread that Nour loved. 'There is no place like this in the whole world,' Nour told him, contemplating the great disorder that surrounded them. 'It is life in all its diversity and inequality, without being domesticated—the children who make the street their school, the beggars who think their life is as dignified as that of the maharajah, the innumerable food stalls without any sanitary control, the constantly honking cars that protest to move forward, and so on. This city is life, combining disorder with energy; all touched with a great freedom. Perhaps, freedom and the lack of the imposition of order are the yin and yang of India—its great quality but also its Achilles' heel.'

After lunch, Hari explained the plan for the next few days, 'Considering the days you told me you could stay, I thought we could take a train trip to Udaipur, Rajasthan, and then drive to Andhra Pradesh to admire its new capital, Amaravati, the new city of the future. That's the best way to understand the dichotomy of the country and the scale of the project I've been commissioned to carry out.'

Early the next morning, they took the train to Udaipur. It was an endless train, with perhaps forty carriages. It was old and lovingly made, but crammed past the point of overflow. The seats, the aisles, and even the deck of each carriage were crowded with people.

Soon, the train picked up speed, and Nour calmly looked out of the window at the landscape of scrubland, hills, and half-constructed buildings everywhere, appearing and disappearing at great speed. Every time they approached a station, the train needed several kilometres to slow down, for the force of the convoy was colossal. You really have to forget everything and trust in fate, thought Nour. 'The tracks are unprotected. At any moment, there may be a fallen tree or a stationary group of animals, and unable to avoid it, the convoy may derail, but, when it happens, it will happen, and life will go on. There is certainly value of life, and it must be respected, for living only in the present also has its advantages.'

In Udaipur, she was fascinated by the work bequeathed by the maharajas. Beauty upon beauty of exquisite proportions. A world now gone that had once risen in grand fashion, combining a crude poverty with a clear refinement as has been the tradition in India. But perhaps in Udaipur, this second quality has won. There was elegance, power, and order in the great palaces built on the rocks. That pyramidal social order where the maharajas stood at the top, had endured for centuries—from the Mongol invasion with the arrival of Babur and the splendour of Emperor Akbar, to the cordial entente with the British East India Company that dominated the country leaving the maharajas with internal power. Throughout this long period, the maharajas developed a taste for order in all facets of life, an attitude reflected in the palace interiors. That order vanished suddenly with the great catharsis of Independence when India underwent its greatest upheaval and transformation, emerging as the world's largest democracy with a new political and social order that brought an end to the power of the maharajahs. But this new path was full of questions. And all the growth that followed bears witness to this.

This is what Hari and Nour talked about that night as they dined in the hotel Hari had booked near the lake. He wanted to explain to her in detail the great project that the Minister of Urban Development had commissioned to him, a project so ambitious that it could impact the future of the country.

'You know well how magnetic, chaotic, uncontrolled, or however you like to define it, life in India is. But I want you to have confidence in its future. I want you to get rid of the sad outlook on this country because of the extent of the disorder and the difficulty in managing it. We are the largest democracy in the world, which has broken with a long tradition of hierarchical submission, and subjugation by foreign powers, such as Afghans, Mongols, Uzbeks, and English who ruled over our territory in successive eras. The organisation into kingdoms under the maharajas abounded in the culture of rule from above. On the other hand, the caste system stratified society, thus perfectly delimiting superiors and inferiors. The advent of democracy has given a new lease on life to a society unaccustomed to complete freedom. And this inevitably translates into constant social upheaval, in the fragility of models and the difficulty of consolidating solid patterns in all fields—culture, urban planning, behaviour, etc.

'It is on this basis that the project of the Ministry of Urban Development is based. It is an attempt to channel the great existing growth because cities and rural areas are growing uncontrollably, and individual taste is imposed without any criteria of harmony. There are no habits or trends that have been consolidated as imperatives, as has happened in other countries in their periods of growth. This was the case in many European countries during the Renaissance, or in America after independence. This has not happened in India. The population, which will soon reach one and a half billion, will have a devastating impact on the landscape and on the lives of the people.

The minister is overwhelmed and believes that only by planning the country's urban development with the help of artificial intelligence can he find a solution to the problem. Just as nature operates with Fibonacci numbers in its expansion, perhaps we can also find algorithmic patterns to order this growth process. It is like identifying a harmonious proportion between the number of houses, distances, their heights, the presence of nature, the ratio of schools, hospitals, hotels, and shops to the number of inhabitants, in city neighbourhoods and emerging towns. The minister does not believe that the solution lies in succeeding in a few one-off projects, such as the new smart city of Amaravati in Andhra Pradesh, which has been planned for almost seven years and is now finally under construction, and will be a beacon of sustainability.

'The challenge calls for a holistic approach that appeals to the whole nation. He believes that the magnitude of the problem requires a global concept that appeals to the whole nation, and he has asked me to find the formula. Once this has been achieved, I would propose a legal reform of land tenure, the crux of the problem, to make it possible,' he explained, not without anxiety.

'I don't know whether to congratulate you, pity you, or worry,' Nour said to him in a sea of doubt, 'for the challenge is so great that it makes one dizzy.'

'Yes,' he said, 'but consider the impact of the project if it succeeded. In the old days, people had little means, which is why they built so little. There was also a rigid order; people built in the areas that the maharajah of each state had at their disposal. Today, people's economy has improved; factories want to invest in new houses, new industries, and new businesses. They do not want to be restricted as to where they can and cannot build, nor do they want to be told what style they must conform to. Hence, the impact on the transformation of the country is enormous and yet chaotic. If we get it right, we will build a great country; if we don't, we will flood it with imbalances and disorder. Think about it; understand the depth of the challenge because if homes and businesses are born anarchically, without aesthetics and connection to each other, the problems will overwhelm us,' he said as he got up from the table to go to rest for the night.

The next day, they started the long road journey to Andhra Pradesh. They left behind the wonder of Udaipur that had once been built orderly.

They began to enter regions where houses sprang up haphazardly, and where there were no drinking water networks, no sewage systems, and no waste collection systems. On the ground, Nour began to understand everything Hari had been explaining at night. In the West and in the Arab tradition, the two cultures which she knew, urbanisation took shape first in villages and then in cities. In that progress, collective services were articulated, such as the arrival of electricity, the construction of roads, the availability of drinking water, the management of waste collection, and the building of schools and hospitals among others. But now she was beginning to realise the magnitude of the challenge in India. During her travels, she saw everything emerging uncontrollably, reflecting a culture that did not obey any pattern. Everyone settled where they could, as they could and, in the absence of rules, as they wanted. 'It is a great challenge,' she thought, 'because, unlike models imposed by an authority, here a dynamic must be created that emerges from the grassroots and takes root among the people. By combining the patterns of aesthetics, the functionality of the buildings, and the calculations of connectivity and economic viability, perhaps we can find the right formula to plan harmonious urban development for the country, just as nature has done.' As she spoke, the car made its way forward, crossing all sorts of obstacles—from local tolls set up on the roads and cows walking undaunted, to pavements that disappeared due to floods and cyclones. As a consequence, the car travelled on dirt tracks full of holes and stones. But, everything oozed a life that emerged spontaneously, unwilling to be encapsulated and structured.

They arrived after three days' journey in Andhra Pradesh. They were awaited by the Governor, who had arranged two rooms in the official government hotel for them. They retired to rest till late in the evening, for the governor had arranged a dinner for them with his close ministers. A man of exquisite taste, he had arranged to dine in the open area in the gardens, beside a small temple. Nour was impressed by the ancient trees whose branches sheltered the table. On either side of them, two large torches cast a beautiful orange light. Soon, dinner began, and the Governor explained his plan in detail:

'The new city of Amaravati will serve as an example of sustainability for India's future smart cities and a reference for the world,' he began proudly. 'A great architect of undisputed prestige is designing the master plan, as well as the official buildings and the main public centres—museums, fairgrounds, universities, theatre, and public parks. Soon, this phase will be completed and, with the infrastructures finished, we will start a public competition for the development of housing projects to create a city of three million inhabitants, whose intelligent configuration will attract talent from everywhere,' he concluded, emphasising the exemplary and open vocation that the new capital of his state would have.

After the introduction, they began to dine. On the table, there were several pots of lamb masala and many bowls of different kinds of hard seeds. The ministers spoke enthusiastically about different aspects of the new city, while serving themselves copious amounts of lamb and pilaf rice. The Governor watched quietly and poured himself only ginger tea and a handful of seeds and nuts. Hari mimicked him, and Nour grimaced in surprise.

'Don't be surprised,' Hari went ahead to tell her, 'many of us in India think that you live longer by eating little.'

'It is true,' said the Minister of Health, 'in India, in many regions there are people who live to be over a hundred years old and are sustained only by water and a few nuts. The body then hardly suffers any wear and tear while processing food and goes on to live in a much more mental way. There is a long tradition of detaching the body from material attachments and using it only as a means of transporting the mind. And the mind appreciates concentration and rest, thereby expending little energy.'

Without looking for it, Nour had just discovered the wisdom of an ancient culture, deeply interested in the power of the mind.

The dinner deepened the relationship of trust with the Governor. Nour congratulated him for his courage to promote such an innovative project, 'I am very impressed by what you are doing, but there are fifty million people living in your state today. In twenty years, there may be seventy million. Amaravati is planned for the next twenty years as a city for three million people to live in. I think, it's valuable for the state to have the newest capital city in the country and the most advanced sustainable city. It's a great message for a nation that has a high regard for nature and understands the value of the planet. But, I worry about the growth of the rest of the state—what kind of buildings will go up, what style of housing will take shape, what order will emerge. Creating a new city under the design of a visionary is fine, but it will be a drop in the ocean. Perhaps you can encourage a popular style throughout the state that will bring about a new order, sow the seeds of a new harmony and root a creative urbanism. I think Hari could work on algorithms to present new models of urbanism for the whole state.'

'I am interested in your vision,' the Governor replied, 'and I really need to think about this. Your vision is modern; it opens doors to the future. We will take it into account.'

The Minister of Culture then intervened to explain the origin of the place where they were dining and the reconstruction works on the nearby temples. Nour did not speak again, for she was satisfied that she had planted the seed.

The next morning, Hari accompanied her to the airport for her departure flight. On the way, they discussed the dinner with the Governor, and Hari thanked her for endorsing his proposal. 'It seemed that the Governor could come up with a complex concept, like addressing the challenge of urban planning using artificial intelligence. Fortunately, he did not take it as an intrusion, but as a new possibility within his grasp.'

Nour replied, 'The challenge in India is crucial because the issue is already upon us—a society in population explosion, without a clear urbanisation model to wisely channel the enormous flow of growth. If the model is not found, it will be a disaster. If it is found, it will be an unprecedented success. And our generation, free from the shackles of tradition and inclined to experiment with artificial intelligence, can achieve it. And you, Hari, can lead it by joining many bright young people. A great challenge for a great task that will undoubtedly change the skin of the country.'

They arrived at the terminal and Hari said goodbye in the Indian way, respectfully with both hands clasped together. Nour was soon lost in the corridors to the boarding lounge. An hour later she was on the Air China flight to Shanghai and from there to her new destination, Dunhuang. She settled into her seat next to the emergency exit, thinking that after the creative chaos of India, she deserved an oasis of calm and perfection. After take-off, she made herself comfortable and soon, lulled by the monotonous noise of the engines, she fell into a deep sleep. In her dream, she returned to the Assembly Hall at United Nations. She was once again absorbed in the debates in the emblematic chamber, where the beauty of art and thought converged, sheltering those who had the power to decide.

Chapter 6

Towards New Health Security

SHE DREAMED that she saw a woman, who had been struggling to subdue the pandemic, take the rostrum. As she slowly made her way to the speakers' platform, the auditorium filled with a thunderous applause. This woman had embodied the strength of lucidity even amidst the most difficult personal circumstances. The virus had completely obliterated one of her lungs and enormously damaged her kidneys and mobility. But she had never given up and, as the head of one of the world's most prestigious research institutes, she had discovered the antivirals to control the pandemic. Like so many other viruses that break out and never quite disappear, the new virus was here to stay, and the best strategy was to control its lethal effects rather than unsuccessfully try to eradicate it. The woman understood this, and without waiting for new possible vaccines, she led her teams to develop antivirals that would block the virus after infection. As she led the research, she reported from her bedside to the world on the progress being made, opening the door to hope.

Today, the whole world, represented in the most powerful agora on the planet, was acknowledging her with that round of applause. She moved at a very slow pace, overcome by a deep emotion on the verge of overflowing. There was a palpable electricity in the atmosphere, an intertwining of expectant gazes awaiting a ground-breaking message.

She began her speech by painting the picture that humanity could not fail to see. 'Today,' she began, 'we have faced a pandemic that has shown us that the planet is a single space, that divisions along borders, ethnicities or civilisations are irrelevant to the risks of survival. Not even the farthest reaches of Asia, Europe, America, Africa, or Australia have been safe from the virus. And despite more than twenty years of waiting for it to arrive, humanity has not been prepared to deal with it. We have had harsh warnings inviting us to prepare, such as bird flu, SARS, and Ebola, but unfortunately, we have not listened to them. And now a virus has stopped the world, though temporarily and with a lower death toll than was predicted because drastic measures could be implemented.

'Friends, citizens of the world,' she said, raising her voice, 'the recent pandemic is the final warning to prepare ourselves for a real health disaster in due course. We must ask ourselves, what would have happened if this virus that has temporarily frozen the planet, had been a virus that killed at the first infection, causing such horrible pains that it would have been a real health disaster?

The world would not have been paralysed; it would have ended up devastated!

'The disease would have spread throughout the whole world causing death of millions. From contagion to death, the journey would have been short. From contagion to cure, there would have been no journey! Hospitals would not have remained places of care, as they could have done little, and everything would have become scarce in a very short time. Panic, not fear, would have taken over everything!

'In the face of such a threat, our only salvation would be neutralising the pandemic-carrying vehicle. And this has failed us now, but it cannot fail us in the future. We must replace the bomb-dropping armies with armies of doctors. On this field we must build a global intervention corps! The first army in the world, paradoxically, should be the army of doctors, the army of peace. Let us give a mandate to the World Health Organisation to transform this healthy clamour into a tangible reality.' Her face was overcome with emotion. The depth of her message immobilised the national delegates, who were more accustomed to discussing strategies than to listening to the profound truths of thinking positively, working together and understanding each other. With a tense expression, she then arrived at the central message, and the entire audience heard her plea in solemn silence, conscious that the outline of the world of the future was being drawn:

'And that army should be dormant while the world is in a state of calm and happiness. But it should be ready to get active as the first warnings of a new infection arrive and the first victims fall on a wretched part of our planet. We must have a decision-making centre that uses artificial intelligence to establish wise methods for collecting accurate data to lead the control of diseases. Of course, we will have to be creative to safeguard privacy while providing sufficient information to the decision-makers to help them draw the right conclusions and generate the right indications. We are a species that has overcome many infections by finding their remedies. But everything has always taken time. Today, acting fast is imperative. Today, the world is innovating more than ever through interconnectedness. Interconnectedness means speed in transmitting knowledge along with the speed in spreading any disease. They are the yin and the yang of the same reality; we cannot renounce the former while trying to protect ourselves from the latter. It is crucial for us to defend ourselves quickly and effectively against any health threat without renouncing interconnection, as this implies deactivating the advances in discovery and knowledge. Defending ourselves by cutting off mobility is disastrous for our future since the route of our progress is through the circuits of connectivity and global mobility. We must therefore rely on our capacity to react faster than a virus can spread. How can we do that?'

Again, there was an electrifying silence in the auditorium.

'Through organising ourselves and leaving behind the old concept of rigid administrations. We must create agile centres equipped with artificial intelligence and recruit the best people to lead them. We should develop a new generation of intellectual property law that combines open use of data with respect for privacy. This is the way forward. A global approach with the best resources and most competent experts, with no country, gender, or cultural quotas, operating under flexible rules to facilitate innovation.

'The World Health Organisation is an excellent starting point, but we must take it to the new dimension. We must turn it into the world's greatest health intelligence centre. We have introduced too many quotas of classic political and administrative balances that lack the leadership in health wisdom that we really need.

'Few of us, today, doubt that NASA is humanity's most advanced centre for space. We should place the World Health Organisation in the same position. It should have an agile and wise team leading it. it should be well connected with all the world's medical research centres, which would use blockchain to send constant data on their treatments, operations, and new research. Therefore, it would be the world's best operating centre for medical data processing and the heart of the best network of specialists in each area. The world's most knowledgeable people could be brought together in a few hours for every potential health threat. We must move to a dynamic and planetary model anchored in future based on knowledge, capacity, and data. All this under a persistent mantra—initiative, initiative, initiative. This way, the appropriate measures can be proposed for each specific place.

'An open and interconnected world is a prosperous world where medicine thrives unobstructed. But it is also a world without physical firewalls and where diseases have wings. The real firewall must be our ability to follow any new disease in detail and to quickly mobilise the best scientists and resources to attack it before it takes flight. We have lacked this today, but we cannot lack it tomorrow.

'This pandemic has also brought us, as with every disaster, a positive seed—prioritising medical research. The big medical companies will be the new corporations on the rise, gathering immense resources to boost their research. We shall soon see great advances in health care, which will open up a new era in disease control.

'I believe that we will win, and thanks to this pandemic, humanity will unite in defence of health for the first time. We have suffered, we have erred, but I hope we have learned. We are one humanity, and we cannot let viruses slip through the state borders, which are always tempted to opt for their own strategies. We must mobilise joint research so that we can be as powerful as possible and agree on a single strategy when necessary. If we act as one humanity, the turmoil we have suffered this time will not happen again,' she concluded. A rainbow was superimposed over the huge screen of the hall framing her face, and the applause of the audience was thunderous again, while she descended the rostrum with assistance.

Chapter 7

To Dunhuang

Deciphering nature's language; discovering new intelligent life

NOUR WOKE up as the plane prepared for a stopover in Shanghai. As the plane approached for landing, she was once again impressed by the growth of that city by the China Sea. This time she would not be able to visit, but her trips in recent years were vivid in her mind. Shanghai represented the new emerging capital of modernity for her. Stealth and futurism were the observations that defined it. With electric cars and motorbikes replacing traditional ones, there was hardly any noise in the streets. Few people still paid with coins, notes, or credit cards because everything was done with QR codes on mobile phones, even handouts! And in this environment that absorbed change and innovation at great speed, millions of people were engaged in a frenetic activity with hardly any conflict or noise. The prevailing order was surprising, as was the rapid spread of artificial intelligence into new domains. Facial recognition had replaced the classic security codes, and citizens could access all procedures digitally, leaving the old bureaucracy behind, though at the cost of being tracked and controlled more easily.

The great debate on the privacy of people in the new world linked to artificial intelligence was spearheaded in Shanghai. Many of her lectures were about this, and the best memories of the congresses came flooding back as the plane flew overhead. The layover was short, and she did not have to change planes. Half of the passengers got off and only a few Chinese citizens got on, wearing protective masks and gloves. The prevention measures there were rigid and exhaustive.

She finally arrived in Dunhuang, in the far east of China, capital of the lands bordering Mongolia. She was eager to thoroughly enjoy the grandeur of Chinese art in the hundreds of caves carved out of the mountain outside the city. She longed to understand the great civilisation. She looked forward to conversations with Xi Tan, the curator of the city's treasures, who was now exploring use of artificial intelligence to discover deeper dimensions of nature. She had met him two years earlier in Dunhuang, during a conference on new lines of thought, and had been impressed by the originality of his ideas. She had tracked him down to spend a few days together to dive into the labyrinth of the caves and calmly contemplate the great art while discussing the new uses of artificial intelligence. Xi Tan had been delighted to welcome her and use the lull in work to focus on new research for the future.

During her first visit to Dunhuang, she was impressed by the beauty of its cave art. How marvellous it was now to discover all those treasures again in the company of those who knew best! More than four hundred caves were carved out of the mountain, a veritable fortress against the vast desert plain, where battles were fought for centuries to stop the Mongol invasion into the interior of China. For over a thousand years, artists painted scenes of the Buddha and fragments of nature using vibrant pigments. A treasure once hidden due to its remoteness, had now been the epicentre of art in the world for over a millennium. The greatness of the treasure overwhelmed her. She wondered how it was possible that the world largely ignored it. She asked herself why she had never heard of Dunhuang until she visited it, and why, unlike the Sistine Chapel or the Parthenon in Athens, Dunhuang was not on the mind of all sentient beings! 'How distant we have been from China lately,' she thought.

Xi Tan had explained to her that, in the face of the ups and downs of Western cultures and the Arab world, China had been a stable and advanced civilisation in the world for more than two millennia, and that its art had been gaining prominence among businessmen and ruling elites. Before the tour of the caves began, Xi told her proudly, 'For more than fifteen hundred years, artists have been recruited in Dunhuang for developing a precious work.

For twenty centuries, until the British came, China was the most advanced civilisation in the world, with art at its centre. That is why a profound harmony pervades all the paintings in these caves.'

Xi was waiting for her at the foot of the plane this time. He wanted to receive her with the utmost deference. On the way to the hotel, they passed by a large pagoda. Xi explained to her the tradition of building them with an odd number of floors. They were a source of inspiration for many poets. She thought that tranquillity and refinement were great qualities of the culture and, in Xi, they also took on the mantle of wisdom.

They left the airport for the high dunes on the other side of the city, where there was a recently opened and successful eco-hotel that Xi had booked. He explained that she would be practically alone in the hotel at the moment, but it would be back in full swing after the pandemic. 'We're still in a strange period now, but I'm sure you'll like it,' he told her. 'You can rest today until sunset, when a guide will accompany you to watch the sunset from the top of the dunes. It is a beautiful sight that you will never forget. You will notice how nature begins to calm down as the wind lifts the smell of dry earth from the strong heat of the day, and the sun bids farewell, painting the horizon red. I will come early tomorrow morning so that we can visit the caves together.'

She rested until the guide came at 6 pm to accompany

her to watch the sunset from the high dunes. What Xi had told her was absolutely true. The smell of dry earth began to permeate everything with a light wind rising up and the earth engulfing the sun, painting the whole horizon a fiery red. Nature was sober but powerful, and the silent force of the desert was felt in all its immensity.

The next morning, Xi picked her up and brought her to the great mountain of four hundred caves.

'Today we will visit most of them. You have already seen some, but you'll discover new things when you look again. It will take time, for each one is a jewel,' he said. 'Just think, it took an artist more than twenty years to complete the cave that the then emperor had commissioned. It was almost fifteen hundred years of precise and unparalleled work!'

Inside the caves, Nour discovered polychromes of great beauty that combined turquoise shades of exquisite green with powerful fire red or intense cobalt blue. It was a great day, and Nour's soul was once again filled with grandeur.

'Seeing this great work of art and the immense work involved, one's confidence in the positive dimension of humanity is restored,' Nour told Xi after the visit.

'True,' he replied calmly, 'art illuminates life, and this place is undoubtedly emblematic of humanity. Now that you know it as well as I do, I'd like to fill you in on my new challenge. I would like to know your opinion to continue the work I am promoting. Your opinion will be crucial to me.'

Nour waited in anticipation of what Xi was about to reveal, a little afraid of the responsibility that he wanted to transfer to her. Without letting her recover from his last words, Xi took her to drink green tea by the ancient tree that closed off the entrance to the last cave.

'The quiet time I enjoy here,' he began, 'has directed my attention to a better understanding of nature, and I have been gradually seduced by its languages which we humans ignore because we do not know the cipher of its codes. For what is language but encrypted communication? Hence, when we do not know a language, when we hear an Indian, a Malay, an Israeli, or a Greek speak without mastering their codes, we understand absolutely nothing, and we only hear a rhythmic song. The same thing happens with the birds who communicate extensively at the beginning and end of the day. We live with them without knowing what they are saying. There is communication between all animals but their sounds seem more like alarms or signals of introduction to me. However, it is fascinating how advanced the communication between birds is. It is very fluid and seems to be as rich in tone as that of humans, so I have undertaken research to decrypt these sounds. If I succeed, I will have access to a new world. It will be a revelation to know what they express, the perspective from which they understand life, and the kind of experiences or information they convey. Perhaps they use new definitions of colours, oflight and its meaning, of the change of the winds or the arrival of the rains. And perhaps they explain to each other what they experience during their flights. I am convinced, birds do not only warn each other of dangers or convey their location while communicating. Many of them act as the ancient troubadours of our cultures, relating experiences and discoveries. Let us not forget that the magical tales of antiquity were always transmitted orally. If I were to discover the code of the language of birds, it would unlock a vital new source of knowledge, opening the door to a new vision of the world.

'But more importantly, we would begin to change man's relationship with the planet. So far, mankind has seen all other beings, be it plants or animals, as inferior entities meant to serve him. Some have even seen them as enemies, and tried their best to distance them or wipe them out. We have little interest in the immense diversity of companions that the planet offers. It has merited no more than a certain curiosity. We are now approaching a significant revolution with the possibility that artificial intelligence will enable us to process innumerable data, decipher multiple communication codes and understand how all entities communicate, discovering new dimensions to everything around us.'

Nour was petrified by Xi Tan's revelation. He had begun by addressing the possibility of accessing a new source of knowledge by decrypting the conversations of birds. From there he had arrived at something much more grandiose—animals, and perhaps the plant kingdom as well, could be having intelligent conversations, and therefore could be much more interesting beings than we had hitherto considered them to be. Going further along this path could lead to something much more grandiose—new perspectives on life and new visions based on different priorities and different ways of fitting into the planet.

'If we succeed in discovering the codes of communication, we could discover new dimensions of countless other companions on the planet,' said Xi. 'We would discover that they have dimensions that we don't know about, and it could transform our lives. Decoding the code of the language of birds is only the first link to go inside nature and explore it with new eyes.'

Nour then understood that although humanity had made great progress in recent decades to preserve nature, it had done so in a limited way—it was limited to having great consideration for nature and to trying to safeguard it. Nature was still seen as an object. Xi Tan was going further. He was opening the door to treating the different forms of nature as intelligent entities experiencing life in their own way. Now, when humanity was thinking about colonising space and going further across the cosmos, it might realise how much it had ignored on its home planet and how much intelligent life had passed by unnoticed.

Suddenly, a double front of immense worlds opened

before mankind—the initially empty outer space, which man was called upon to explore and colonise; and the teeming world of life on the home planet, whose profound sophistication he had been unaware of for millennia.

'What a colossal challenge, and how much work remains to be done! Now I understand the magnitude of the challenge that you're talking about,' Nour said. 'And it is true that artificial intelligence can help mankind fundamentally to deal with it. After all, its strength lies in deciphering codes and understanding complex processes that can be reduced to series. What man could not decipher directly with his brain, he will accomplish with the brains that he and she will set in motion.'

'I'm glad you don't think it's crazy,' Xi told her, 'because this is a virgin field, and we need the new generation to take it over and develop.'

Nour shivered as she visualised how much positive work was still left to do and discover. Nevertheless, she also perceived the shadow of destruction looming large with the potential to overpower everything. She understood the great danger posed by a few with their primitive will to dominate, which could end up ruining everything. She trusted that the shadow would fade, but the mere feeling froze her breath, as if she had been struck by a gust of icy wind. Knowing Xi's quiet soul, she found the memory of all those driven only by the primitive dimensions of humanity, domination and hatred, hateful. She thought, 'the linear, simple life that has been part of our history up till now is no longer of interest. We must quickly move into the new phase of unlocking the talent to harvest the proliferation of new contributions, as I have come to experience today with Xi.'

Gradually, she recovered and sipped the cup of green tea. She even laughed as she listened to Xi's amusing anecdotes about the experiences of other visitors.

In the end, she was overcome by a deep euphoria. She felt she had made the right decision in returning to Dunhuang and reconnecting with a civilisation as exquisite and cultivated as China's. The last hundred years had been hard for the country before Deng Xiaoping set it on the right track. Nonetheless, China had always been the gateway to higher things. Now, in the age of artificial intelligence, it was opening the door to the great inner dimensions of all the other living beings on the planet. What a great challenge, but, above all, what a great task for her generation!

The next day Xi Tan accompanied her to the airport for her departure flight. She was leaving Dunhuang, looking at the world with new eyes. She knew that it would take time for Xi's advance to gain momentum, but she was sure that a new north had been set. From now on, this would be a priority in the development of the intelligence systems, a field in which she could significantly contribute. 'What a great change could come about in the relationship with all beings on the planet,' she thought as she said goodbye to Xi. He smoothly escorted her through the checkpoints and left her at the door of the plane. Shortly, she took off for Novosibirsk. During that long trip she would unravel the immensity of the new task, remember the beauty of the cave art, and think about how open the future was and how much humanity still had to discover. With the thrumming of the plane's engines, she fell asleep and entered a deep state of reverie.

Chapter 8

Towards A Clean World

NOUR AGAIN found herself following the debate on the future of the world. The room was buzzing, for the young woman whose arms were tattooed with winds and hands were carved with the moon and the sun, was about to speak. Her soul trembled, but she began her speech with a firm look at the delegates. At the age of twenty-five, she stood before the large audience as a member of what was already being called the 'covid generation', representing a dense swarm of environmental organisations. Her judiciousness did not undermine what was to be a memorable speech, thanks to the mixture of sadness and hope that her words brought out.

'I belong to a generation that was just beginning to hope for better times than those that preceded us. My youth urges me to speak in direct words that indicate excitement while springing from fear. You will notice in my tone the freshness and perhaps the naivety of young people who dream of the future. Our scars are still tender, almost raw, for as a generation that has seen its time stopping right at the point of blossoming, I bear an early imprint of the gravity marking my words.

'We have inherited from our predecessors a keen awareness of the fate of the planet. We have heard the clamour getting intense each year for a cleaner, more sustainable world, without melting ice, deforestation, and increasing pollution. We love animals, clean air, green mountains, blue seas, crystalline rivers, and nature as an example of diversity, with millions of beings freely reproducing under a precise and extraordinary biological clock. We love the beauty of this planet, and we want all men and women to join the fight for its preservation.

'But, unlike the young people who raised the green flag at the dawn of the century, we do not want to go back on anything; we do not want to replace the car with the bicycle or the airplane with the train. On the contrary, we want to accelerate progress to overcome weaknesses. We have witnessed the deep depression that comes from halting the rapid march of the planet. It will be said that those were months, and not moments. But I ask you, what are a few months in the long evolution of our civilisation? Moments and only moments. These moments of paralysis have led to a deep fear and a profound disorder because they have created mistrust and uncertainty. The wheel of progress has turned backwards, and the devastation has been colossal. That is why we want to move forward to learn how to protect the environment through invention, new technology, and the creative dynamism of people.

'My generation represents the determination to move forward, not the enthrallment of stillness. We want to be inheritors of the advice Ulysses received in the most decisive moment of his long voyage to Ithaca, when the goddess whispered in his ear, the bolder a man is, the more fortune he achieves in his endeavours. Yes, wise delegates, at this turning point in history, we must be the generation of audacity to bring fortune to humanity.'

Resounding applause echoed through the hall, a clear sign of admiration for someone so young but so determined to overcome everything and to look for light through the cracks of a paralysing darkness.

With new energy, she continued, 'We want to advance in the preservation of the planet, not by following the path of renunciation but by accelerating innovation. How painful are those seas full of plastics and waters blackened by unchecked waste! How sad are those fish poisoned by the pesticides flooding the oceans! How agonising it is to see the big cities covered with a thick layer of pollution that deprives them of the clear blue sky and the sun! How sad it is to see thousands of open dumps in so many corners of the planet, smoking and stinking, where the sources of future diseases accumulate and where the stench chases life away!

'Our present civilisation unfailingly wants a world in which nature is restored to its full splendour, in which man and woman are their own best advocates, and we ardently desire to face this course immediately. Only if we make new discoveries leading to new efficient recovery technologies will we succeed in restoring nature's cleanliness.

'Only Then can we ensure the purity of the seas and the continuity of the glaciers!

'The challenge is faced by humanity as a whole. This is why we ask to move forward in building a new global political architecture, just as the man we look up to declared at the opening of our great assembly. We must set the course that will guide our ship to the right port!

'My generation wants to navigate the waters of knowledge and invention. We want to get to the other side of the river, to the side of the clean planet, through the advances of technology. We have seen the suffering that can be caused by stopping the planet even momentarily, and we don't want to stop it for long. That would destroy our future and jeopardise all our dreams. Our generation has understood the importance of time in moving forward in a sustainable world. We do not want false ideas that reverse our progress; we want to triumph by the force of progress!

'That's why, I ask you to make rules so that we can take action, and not hold ourselves back; to make laws so that we can create, not give up! We want a grand alliance of scientists, governments, entrepreneurs and inventors to overcome pollution and prevent the destruction of the environment. Let us move forward not only to save, but to improve our planet; let us use invention to drive technological progress forward at a faster pace.

'We do not believe in the idyllic, but we do believe in the power of science, and in man's ability to innovate and surpass his own ideas,' she said.

'If the previous generation faced a crisis at the beginning of the century and survived it with a certain resignation, my generation wants to demonstrate its capacity for recovery equal to the intensity of the blow it has suffered. We want to accelerate everything that breathes solutions, relates to innovation, and points to the triumph of intelligence. We are a generation that gives wings to creation and innovation. We want to be a strong generation that seeks victory over risks through daring and invention while defending and preserving our planet. We want you to legislate in favour of multiplying incentives and supporting those who discover and invent. The idealistic songs of yesterday do not seduce us. The future attracts us like a magnet with its power and capacity. Let us make this great dream come true, together and for all.'

Before saying goodbye, she projected images of the latest inventions which, though completed, are still unknown in everyday life—airplanes flying with solar energy, cities illuminated by the winds, desalinated sea water irrigating the deserts and making the vegetation flourish, and so on. There were dozens of images that made the audience move quickly from incredulity to conviction.

Chapter 9

To Novosibirsk

The arbitration power of artificial intelligence

IT WAS a long flight in the old propeller-powered Tupolev, which linked Dunhuang with Novosibirsk, the city of science in Russia. She was impressed by the untouched nature she flew over. She thought about how much humanity could comfortably fit there, rethinking the fallacy of the theories of overpopulation. 'We need to organise our spaces well instead of limiting our growth,' she said to herself with conviction. 'It's all about being intelligent. If we make effective use of our new connectivity and organise ourselves better under a new political architecture, nothing should prevent us from supporting well-planned human settlements and a wiser distribution of humanity on the planet. She continued to look out of the airplane window for hours, and the idea of transforming spaces became more and more cherished.

She had been to Novosibirsk once, and the depth of the discussions in the city of science made her stay brief

She had always wanted to return, but her other pressing commitments prevented her from doing so. Now, with the suspension of congresses and conferences all over the world, she had found the time to immerse herself in that hive of knowledge, accepting the invitation of the president of the Academy of Sciences, Dimitry Zhukov.

As the plane descended, she remembered her first trip. She had visited that tiny fortress of knowledge, in the middle of Siberia, early in her career. She had flown from Moscow and landed at night on an icy runway. She had flown over thousands of fir trees for hours without any houses or villages, crossing a large part of Siberia from the Russian capital. It was a wilderness of endless immensity, exuding tranquillity in its monotony and clarity of colours. The plane glided over the icy runway before stopping smoothly. This landing, at thirty degrees below zero, impressed her. Stepping out of the Tupolev, she noticed the purity of the air. She could breathe pure oxygen. The cold air was so dry that it didn't hurt to breathe it—an unparalleled sensation that she would never forget. She had then walked from the foot of the plane to the terminal accompanied by two burly employees who held her to prevent her from slipping, and she was surprised that the cold hardly affected her. She vividly remembered the power she had felt on her first trip—she, born in the hottest region of the planet, was at the epicentre of the cold, facing it with a smile. This gave her a feeling of triumph and enormous security.

On her last visit, she had understood much of the Russian soul, its determination, courage, and capacity to resist and face the greatest adversities with a noble outlook. The city of Novosibirsk was a proof of this. It gained importance when, during Hitler's invasion in the Second World War, the Soviet power decided to make it the capital of the armaments industry because of its distance from the front. A small city of thirty thousand inhabitants suddenly had half a million in a few months.

It manufactured essential armaments to supply to the troops, helping to resist the invasion which the heavy snowfalls had temporarily slowed down. Despite facing invasion from a well-armed army and having no means at its disposal, Russia did not surrender and decided to resist. Hitler's treacherous coup, which unilaterally broke the non-aggression pact, failed thanks to Russia's profound determination. Novosibirsk, with its enclave in the most impregnable part of Siberia, was the forge of armed resistance. When the war was over, it was decided that it would be turned into the City of Science, as a token of recognition for the feat accomplished. The Soviet power kept the scientists well isolated and focused on their research. Hence, the city experienced a second wave of growth, from half a million to a million inhabitants, and became the spearhead of scientific research in the East.

The Russian government promoted it and urged it to

host foreign leaders who wanted to strengthen relations. Thus, great Western political leaders of the sixties, such as President De Gaulle, visited it in the middle of the Cold War. This was the era of the space race, and Novosibirsk was the best showcase of Soviet scientific power and capabilities.

Dimitry Zhukov, president of the Academy, was Nour's host on this visit. Recently, they had written much as he and his wife, Anastasia, advanced their research into the application of artificial intelligence systems in traffic management. They were at the forefront of the artificial intelligence program to regulate land mobility in Russia. A radar and visual recognition system would arbitrate the trajectory of cars. He had been commissioned by the political authorities to carry out this research considering the high road accident rate in the country.

Dimitry always wrote to Nour with great precision about his research. He was now studying how to arbitrate in borderline situations and unavoidable accidents that could unfold differently depending on who bore the impact. Today, data holds enormous knowledge and information about all the people involved in a presumed crash, enabling crises management from new angles. To explain the new world we were entering, Dimitry had presented a junction where accidents would inevitably occur and outlined a specific case that visualised the new developments in decision-making.

The stakes were high. One specific scene made this clear. A long avenue crossed a city. An old couple was walking on a sidewalk, on the pedestrian crossing there were two children about to cross without looking. Coming towards them was a high-speed car that would either swerve or run them over dramatically. There were three possible scenarios—the car would brake unsuccessfully and run over the children; it would swerve to the left and run over the elderly couple; or it would swerve to the right, hit a lamppost and kill the driver. The artificial intelligence regulator system was supposed to act and impose one of the three situations. The system provided an enormous amount of data on all the people involved and combined it quickly to make a more informed decision than any human could ever imagine. The system knew that the woman had just been awarded a Nobel Prize for Medicine, was perfectly healthy, and was developing highly advanced research to create a drug against tick bites that caused meningitis in the Altai region and in large forested areas of the planet. All this made her a person with a great multiplier coefficient of importance to humanity. It also knew that one of the two children had incurable leukaemia and would inevitably die in less than a year. The other child was naturally very agile and had a good chance of reacting with great reflexes on being run over.

It also knew that the driver was a prestigious neurosurgeon who was driving faster than the speed limit, making him initially guilty of what was going to happen and ready to sacrifice himself. He was tired because he had been operating on the Governor of the region all night, after a serious stroke he had suffered at the end of a tense government meeting following the Moscow-imposed decision to close the main mines that provided massive employment in the region.

Dimitry wanted to discuss with Nour how to combine the value of each of the components of the algorithm. His mission was to organise the complexity of the decision rationally, replacing fate. Man could decide now. What was more impressive was that the decision could be taken in milliseconds after processing many disconnected variables. But to do so, the system needed to have modulated beforehand the value of each one of the variables.

As a courtesy, Dimitry Zukhov went to pick her up at the airport and brought her a small bouquet of flowers. In Russia, the way guests were received was still important, and flowers were never lacking for someone who was appreciated. Nour was doubly grateful to him for his attentions, both for coming to fetch her personally and for receiving her with flowers. There was something grand in the Russian soul that touched her deeply. She liked the fact that a passion for science and life converged in the Russian character. She had felt it the first time she was there, and she sensed that she would feel it deeply once again.

From the airport they went to the hotel that Dimitry

had arranged for her in the northern part of the city, surrounded by nature. There Anastasia was waiting for them to have lunch on the terrace overlooking the lake. Anastasia was very happy to meet Nour. Dimitry had told her about Nour, and Anastasia had imagined Nour like her daughter, who had moved to Moscow several years ago and was at the helm of one of the most prestigious eye research teams as a surgeon. Having suffered hardships and limitations for much of her life because of communism, she was enthusiastic about what the new generation could now do and how quickly they were achieving their goals.

As soon as Nour sat down at the table, Dimitry ordered some blinis with caviar and a bottle of ice-cold vodka.

'I think you're hungry after your trip. While they bring us lunch, let's have this as an aperitif,' he said in good humour. As the vodka was poured, they toasted to sharing a brilliant few days together and began to chat.

'I've been poring over the information you sent me,' Nour began. 'Very interesting and decisive, too! The case places a great responsibility on mankind in deciding the fate of others. But it is true that knowing all the details of situations can lead to more intelligent handling of accidents. The correct assignment of values to the components at stake is essential for the correct configuration of the system.'

'Exactly,' said Dimitry. 'And, what is your perception?'

'In the concrete case of the accident at the crossroads,

I first thought of an assignment of coefficients to discuss them openly today. For example, we can give the value of 10 to a young life, 6 to an adult life, and 2 for old age, 2. Similarly, 10 to complete health, 6 to fragile health, and 0 to health leading to certain death. A value of 10 to the work that positively benefits more than a million people, 6 to that which reaches between a hundred thousand and a million people, 4 to that which only affects between a thousand and ten thousand people, 2 to that which affects between a hundred and a thousand people, and 0 to that which affects less than a hundred people.' She continued this way, going through the possible values of the many variables at play. 'But this would act as a starting point,' she added. 'According to experience and the cases arbitrated, we could enable the system to introduce new variables with weighting of values. The system would develop and enrich itself in the future. This is the value of artificial intelligence. Not only can it compute more efficiently than man, but it can learn from its own experience and create its own programs and future solutions. In the case of the accident, the sum of the values would suggest sacrificing the sick child—contrary to what would have been chosen without the arbitration of artificial intelligence. This is because limited knowledge about the actors in play would have suggested sacrificing the surgeon.'

'I find your thoughts very interesting and valuable; above all, I think it is essential to design a function that allows the system to modulate according to the results. In Russia, we have a high accident rate, and we need to be able to deter the biggest risk-takers. Illegal conduct needs to have highly decisive coefficients, and the system needs to be sensitive to processing its impact and implementing new deterrent initiatives,' said Dimitry. 'And since you found this case interesting, I'll tell you another one. What if an approaching asteroid were to hit the Earth, and we could divert it to avoid a densely populated city, but instead make it strike a cluster of villages in the countryside? The new victims would be condemned by human choice, while the legion of dead in the city would be so by the effect of fate.

'Do you think it is possible to act, or will those who execute the change be accused of committing a crime by the families of the new victims?'

'It is certainly a case of our new age,' said Nour. 'It touches upon the idea of overcoming natural destiny and taking charge of history. It is full of virtues as well as risks. Especially if, in the end, the decisions are made by a leader and not by the collective. This way we may be opening the door to a new domination of man by man. This is an exciting subject for everyone working on the limits of the use of artificial intelligence, something the new generation will have to work on extensively. We will have to involve philosophers in new research, develop a moral component for the new era, and incorporate it into the programs. The component needs to be sufficiently deep, without being constricting, to set limits that cannot be transgressed, but not get entangled in small details. In the case that you mention, I think, it should be decided to save the city and to classify the hecatomb as an inevitable accident, since man has not caused it, but has limited its damage by redirecting it.'

As they relished the dessert, their conversation turned to life in Novosibirsk, with Dimitry and Anastasia telling a thousand stories of their scientific colleagues. The vodka had worked its tongue-loosening effect, and soon Nour got well acquainted with the ins and outs of the place. In the middle of the afternoon, Dimitry and Anastasia left Nour to rest and arranged to pick her up early the next morning to take her to see the Academy.

It was the beginning of several days of intense work and rich discussions. Everyone was becoming increasingly aware that humanity was now entering a much more complex era, as it took control of its destiny based on a thorough knowledge of all the elements of the given situation. Earlier, humanity had lived as a child, now it was beginning to live as an adult. As a child, it took many things for granted in an innate lack of awareness. It ignored much and doubted little. Now, as an adult, it would be aware of the risks, and it would arbitrate sensibly in the face of conflicts, but it would be weighed down by the gravity of the decisions. Although everything would become fairer, everything would also lose the freshness and excitement that only oblivion and ignorance can give. Humanity was beginning to calibrate the weight and gravity of all actions. And there was no turning back. Once it developed the capacity to know more and to process enormous data relating to each of us at dizzying speed, it would no longer be possible to return to the age of innocence.

'We may have wanted to attain knowledge, but once we have attained it, it will possess us; we will not be able to renounce it. It is impossible to ignore the new world we are entering. Knowledge is emerging as a new dominant being, and it will be my generation's responsibility to use it wisely. We must configure its limitations carefully so that no one can abuse it and turn us into objects of a superior game. It is certainly a great field to develop,' thought Nour. She marvelled, not only at the rigour and discipline of the Russian scientists, but also at their intense emotionality hidden under an initial layer of coldness.

Her friendship with Dimitry and Anastasia grew. On the last day, they invited her for dinner in one of the traditional taverns, a large wooden hut, where Russian songs were played to the sound of the balalaika. They dined on traditional borscht, salmon roe, and beef Stroganoff with wild mushrooms. As the evening progressed, the songs got louder and louder, and everyone clapped along with a sip of ice-cold vodka. The atmosphere became intimate as everyone there became one big family, intoxicated by the magic of the moment. After an hour, their eyes sparkling with excitement and alcohol, and when the musicians played the song *Kalinka*, Constantin, a strong, slender young man with a face full of power and vitality, who danced forward on his heels with his knees bent, approached Nour and asked her to dance. Everyone encouraged her, and she found herself instantly adapting to Constantin's rhythm. The deep romantic charge of the traditional Russian music and the young man's energy awakened her sensuality. Her hips began to sway and her dance became charged with electricity. As he held her hand at every turn, she felt his pulse. It was amazing how quickly she felt deeply connected with a stranger. She felt surprisingly close! The connection grew stronger as they danced, and the musicians played more and more eagerly.

Nour's Arabic roots were revealed in all their intensity, displaying an irresistible sensuality that lasted all night long. She danced as she hadn't danced in a long time and, in the midst of a turn, Constantin put his hand around the back of her neck and brought his lips close to hers. 'You are as beautiful as a shooting star, and your kisses must be as delicious as the nights of the full moon,' he said before looking at her lovingly, kissing her. She basked in the feeling of pleasure seeping into her. Without seeking it, Nour surrendered to the young man's seduction and thus began one of the most beautiful nights of her life.

There is a wonderful aspect to the Russian soul, its immediate acceleration towards intensity. There is no point between the first encounter and the highest point of a relationship—it is reached instantaneously, to the rhythm of an intuitive complicity. One could say that the door is open to the essentials of life and Chronos becomes unequivocal. No one needs time to decide because the connection travels faster than time does. And that is what Nour experienced that night.

So, when it was closing time and the musicians prepared to leave, she knew what she had to do, tell Dimitry and Anastasia that she would see them the next morning, and let herself be carried away by Constantin. And it happened just like that, without the need for false explanations. And this is perhaps the second great characteristic of the Russian soul—you can get to the heart of every situation without beating around the bush. So much time has been wasted in the long years of sterile communism that no one today wants to unnecessarily waste even a second of their short existence.

Nour let herself be carried away by Constantin's vitality and spent the night making love in his small dacha. It was a surprising and unexpected encounter in which she exceptionally felt the passion of the Russian soul.

In mid-morning of the following day, she went to Dimitry's house. They had arranged to meet to say goodbye. Her face reflected both joy and sadness.

Everything had happened too quickly, and perhaps too intensely, but one is never left indifferent on delving into the intimacy of the Russian soul. Dimitry, in turn, was pleased that the stay had been so fruitful. He accompanied her to the airport, and lovingly dedicated to her his latest book that had just been published in English. It had a very intriguing title: *Does the Universe Have Limits?* Nour promised to start reading it on the plane and to send him her comments soon.

The airport was small, and she easily passed all the checkpoints. Soon, she was in the sky again, this time on her way to Samarkand. She had spent most of the night awake, and now, in the tranquil flight, she felt really tired. Sleep took hold of her again and, without delay, carried her back to the hall of the Palais des Nations where the great discussion on the new political architecture of the world continued in great intensity.

Chapter 10

Towards The End Of Weapons

AND THEN the man, for whom nothing really seemed impossible, spoke.

'I have come to speak to you,' he began, tucking his black-rimmed spectacles between his thick eyebrows, 'about what we all know, but to which we have not yet reacted as we should. As humanity, we are sitting on a powder keg, which, on exploding, will be uncontrollable and plunge mankind into the darkest times it has ever known.

'We live in a world that harbours the greatest weapons of mass destruction, loaded and aimed at specific targets, but in silence, because fear and fate have been with us until now. As President of the United Nations Conference on Disarmament, I am confronted with this tragic helplessness—to know the level of destruction with which we have endowed ourselves while feeling the inability to redirect it, to put an end to this evil dream which will one day end in our annihilation. That is why I am called the man for whom nothing is really impossible. Every measure, every initiative that I propose to those adding to the bad dream, always becomes irrelevant in the face of the frenzied race to develop something new and even more devastating. It is like Penelope's constant weaving and unweaving while waiting for Ulysses. Progress is made only to be retraced again by the irruption of a new and even more sophisticated weapon that will have to be banned. And then again a new one will appear which, since it is not regulated, will once again require to be controlled collectively by means of a negotiated prohibition and, in the meantime, there is always the open window of destruction. As a result, the world's capacity for annihilation continues to grow.

'And so, we live with a reality that presents the darkest faces humanity can imagine. As the Stockholm International Peace Research Institute has identified, today we have more than fifteen thousand nuclear warheads stockpiled and ready to be launched. Two nuclear bombs were enough to end a World War in 1945. Do you realise what it means to have more than ten thousand today? Do you realise the destruction this means? And, do you realise the danger that the existence of multiple actors in play also adds? Because if at first there were two and then five, now there are already nine and two more on the way who ride on the sly to become members of a perverse club with entrances, but no exits!

'At the time, the terrible dream of the First World War led to two great demons, chemical and biological weapons, being reduced and progressively eliminated under the 1925 Geneva Convention. Since then, we have not let our guard down, and two major international legal norms hold these two crooked-headed monsters well locked.

'The 1972 Biological Weapons Convention (BWC) and the 1993 Chemical Weapons Convention (CWC) are the two cells of the monsters with twisted heads, and a good guardian, the International Committee of the Red Cross, ensures that they are permanently enforced.

'And this virus has shown openly the value of the work done. A virus of a single type has momentarily frozen us. The biological or chemical weapons that today's armies might have at their disposal would produce a multitude of viruses capable of causing atrocious deformities, death, and immediate suffering. This virus has shown us that our civilisation wants to experience the positive development of science and to advance in all creative aspects of the planet. Therefore, these destructive and annihilating dynamics must be definitively eradicated.

'The pandemic has made it clear that we cannot take on any great disorder without causing serious damage to everyone. A small virus has changed the way we come into contact with one another, has brought down all the world's airlines and major car factories, broken all the production and distribution chains in countless sectors, and put the ordinary lives of millions of people out of kilter. Can you imagine what would have happened if, instead of one virus, dozens of viruses had broken out, spread by multiple bombs at the same time? Can you imagine?'

All the faces were tinged with gravity, as if the image of desolation and pain of a world swept by biological warfare had crossed the mind of every delegate for an instant. A deep silence thus fell over the room.

And, like a sharp spear, the speaker hurled the answer, 'The world would go to hell; we would go back to the caves to try to survive the longest winter of centuries and centuries for mankind. 'We' is perhaps not the right word here. 'They' is a more appropriate term because at least I would not be in that group. Better to perish than to begin a life in which evil formations, death amidst terrible sufferings, and great misery would be constant. Everyone, including those who would have activated the curse, would be a loser from this perverse action. Although we know this theoretically, we have not made it palpable to the world in a way that humanity assumes it as its highest priority. If people understood that what we have suffered is only one percent of what we would suffer if a chemical, biological, or nuclear war were to break out, perhaps then we could say that we are on the true path of humanity's progress!

'Today, thanks to this small visualisation of the evil that the devastating pandemic has presented before us, I can take the floor, no longer in front of the experts trying to contain the unnatural experience of the arms race, but before you, the representatives of the whole world. And I say firmly and loudly, the time has come to act, to prioritise creating a global political architecture that enables us to deactivate these arsenals and submit them to the control of a body that guarantees their safe non-use. This would be a body that could use them to ward off any possible future invasion by beings from other galaxies, in case we have to defend ourselves. And, in that case, we could wield them to show what we are capable of creating and what we are capable of having.

'This new world has many areas in which to act under a new vision. But I would like to ask you to set priorities, and, in my opinion, the top priority must be to identify a new global political architecture that will decisively neutralise the risk of wars. Just as a small virus that uncontrollably emerged in a specific place has paralysed us all on the five continents, a small war can unleash a catastrophe of major proportions.

'We live in a world in which intelligence must take precedence; resorting to force returns us to being entities of primitive behaviour. Acting like brutal beings in an interconnected and increasingly technological world leads us to the unacceptable risk of suffering devastating dynamics. Better to end this risk today. I ask you to understand that bombs are the result of conflicts between groups and that, to eliminate the effect, the cause must be eliminated. Only by overcoming the divisions in the form of nations and civilisations, and by placing our centre of gravity on man as such, will we be able to block the emergence of confrontational dynamics. That is why, I welcome the Secretary-General's appeal and trust that this extraordinary event will enable us to understand the gravity and fragility on which we are based and the urgency of reversing the situation.

'Let us make it our top priority to put an end to the risk of war. It is the greatest of the dangers that beset us. And, let us put an end not only to its means, weapons, but also to its breeding ground and nourishment, the division of mankind into nations.

'And so, the seed we are now planting will germinate. We will create a global culture of peace that will close the way for some madmen or some intelligent, but overly egotistical, beings to destroy us, believing they can rule as new emperors over a subjugated world. Because, if this happens, there will be no world, nor will the supposed emperor have any court, nor any life worth living!' And thus, he concluded his speech bluntly, and for the first time, some began to call him the most needed man, the one whom all wished to see triumph.

Chapter 11

Along The Silk Road

The exploration of the cosmos, the power of sound and the transformation of education.

THANKS TO the close relationship between Russia and Uzbekistan, there was a weekly direct flight between Novosibirsk and Samarkand. Technicians from the two major national companies regularly travelled to share data, experiences, and strategies. Nour took advantage of this route, which was mostly used by these employees.

After take-off, the plane flew over Central Asia on its way to Samarkand. From there, she would first reach Istanbul retracing the path of the ancient Silk Road, and then Athens. She was fascinated by the oriental dimension that united all those cities, once hosting the peaks of civilisations. All of them had played such an important role in the flourishing history of the world!

The journey through valleys of deep vegetation and long, impassable deserts would have been insurmountable by land. But the trip by plane through that clear sky did not seem excessively long. She marvelled at the great leap of humanity in overcoming by air the geographical barriers erected by nature. Its intelligence for acquiring a dimension that was not innate—flying.

'As human beings,' she thought, 'we can get along in the other environments, land and water. We will never be able to run or jump like a tiger or cross the ocean like a dolphin, but we can move in both environments. In the air, nature has given us no ability. And yet, with our intelligence, we have become the fastest bird that can travel the greatest distance. A great paradox of destiny. We have managed to take the most advanced position. What bird can fly at a thousand kilometres an hour, or fly for fifteen thousand kilometres without stopping? We are the only ones, even though we do it not with our limbs but rather inside the womb we have built. In short, we have paraphrased the famous thought of Archimedes of Syracuse, "Give me a fulcrum and I will raise the Earth." We have said, "Give me a problem and we will give you the solution", because we have a solid foundation of ideas.' After a long nap, Nour had woken up in a good mood and was thinking about the privilege of travelling for miles while comfortably sitting above the clouds. When the pilot announced the start of the descent, she drained her coffee and relaxed by rereading the chapter on the adventures of Hassan al-Basri in *One Thousand and One Nights*, her favourite book, to immerse herself in the maze of Central Asia.

Samarkand welcomed her with the unmistakable smell of dry earth mixed with the sweet aroma of its abundant fig and carob trees. The jewel of the past, the capital of the junction of East and West when the great Tamerlane created the largest empire in Central Asia, continued to be a significant place.

It had been a major centre of astronomical calculation and observation for centuries, and great scholars, such as Ulugh Beg and Ali Qushji, had conducted their research there. People here had always been fascinated by the study of the stars. Moreover, their religious tradition never had a reductionist conception of the earth as the centre of everything. There was always a passion for the universe. While in the Christian West, scholars had to risk their lives to study the sun or the planets, harassed by the relentless persecution of the religious hierarchies, the Islamic East had opened doors to seek the secrets of the cosmos. Thus, great sages of the past lived in Samarkand and Bukhara, and left the tradition of the study of astronomy deeply rooted. Since then, the city had regularly attracted great scientists to research the stars.

Aziz, perhaps the most respected astronomer in the world at the time, was waiting for Nour. He lived in an old traditional Uzbek-style wooden house next to the Bibi Khanum mosque. She had met him two years ago, during the International Astronomy Congress, where he had been made president of the International Astronomical Union. At the congress she had presented a highly acclaimed paper on algorithms for exploring the cosmos. They had become friends after he announced that he would henceforth devote his efforts to the confluence of human knowledge and artificial intelligence in exploration of the universe. They had yet to meet to discuss how to move forward on this path. Now, due to the pause caused by the pandemic, the opportunity had arisen.

Already in his eighties, Aziz looked like the reincarnation of the great mathematicians of the golden age of science in Islam—white beard, large hands and warm, brown, almond-shaped eyes. He had a calm and elegant manner that helped one to quickly forget the swirl of everyday life. Being with him was like entering the hall of the humanity's greatness.

He received Nour with joy and sent his assistant, Gulnara, to bring the mint tea and nut sweets that had been prepared to welcome her. Nour, in turn, gave him some Novosibirsk matryoshkas, painted with large faces on golden backgrounds. They talked a little about the lockdown, which had also reached Samarkand, and in the evening, they went to the courtyard where dinner was prepared with the traditional Uzbek pilaf.

'What were you thinking of when you spoke of incorporating artificial intelligence into the discovery of the universe?' Nour asked him as they served themselves.

'That we will enter adulthood in exploring the stars with it,' he told her. 'Today, we already know that the universe is far more immense than any mind can dream or imagine, and its grandeur surpasses anything we can calculate. Only with the new generation of computerised brains, which can solve algebraic operations at breakneck speed, will we be able to enter the infinite without getting lost. Moreover, thanks to the robots, we will be able to advance in the exploring the outer frontiers of our galaxy and navigate the open skies of the universe. Robots will be able to navigate for hundreds of years to transmit all the information we need on what is going on in the farthest reaches of the cosmos. We human beings have reached the limit of what we could do ourselves, to understand that the universe exceeds our solar system and as many galaxies as we can see. After confronting this challenge, we have decided not to stop. From here, we must wisely use our intelligence to piggyback on new technologies.'

'I am glad that a man like you,' said Nour, 'born when even the most elementary computer did not exist, and absorbed all his life in the books of the great astronomers of the past, should have such a vision of the future and such blind confidence in the new creatures of humanity.'

'Don't think it so strange,' Aziz replied. 'It's good to recognise what empowers us and frees us from limitations. Artificial intelligence is an arm that reaches out where our limbs do not. I believe in its power to process and in our ability to create new intelligences and to keep them under our control. I tell you this from my heart—today is a great day for me. It fills me with happiness that you have come. To me, you are the one who is taking the baton of the new dimensions of research. You are the one who can communicate the magnitude of the challenge we are facing and encourage new generations to take it up. You can motivate the young to make this one of their life projects, a contribution in golden letters to the progress of humanity.'

It was emotional and moving. Aziz's words struck a chord with Nour.

'The two directions to which you have referred,' she said, 'calculating the magnitude of the universe and exploring it with replicants, are certainly fabulous contribution of artificial intelligence to our future. And, as you say, we are planting the seed for man to start diving into the vastness of the universe.'

They talked for hours and hours that night, thus beginning what would be a few unforgettable days during which Nour exquisitely combined discovering the beauty of the world's ancient jewel with exploring the future. In the morning, her spirit was lost in the wonders of the past—the madrasas, the carpet and pottery shops, the small houses, and the spice warehouses with jute sacks of saffron and cumin by the doors, which immersed her in the old world of the caravanserais, the union of East and

West, which not only transported spices but also ideas and customs. It was there that *One Thousand and One Nights*, the greatest book of the human imagination, was written. It was there that Roxana, the wife of Alexander the Great, was born. She would accompany him to Ashgabat, the city of love in Turkmenistan, at the foot of the mountains of Kopet Dag, to begin the invasion of Persia. There had reigned the great Tamerlane, who had gathered an army of more than four hundred thousand men and knew how to move it across the great steppes of Central Asia to reach the Indian Ocean and onto India.

And, at night, her spirit flew with Aziz on the paths of the future.

They spent three passionate days together, and as the last evening came to an end, Nour embraced him tenderly. His body was pure spirit, for his arms and shoulders were barely strong, but his eyes still shone with life, seeking to understand why the universe was so immense and what its inscrutable confines held. That night, Nour told him,

'I really thank you for enlightening me on how much we can still discover and use artificial intelligence to advance the universe. From what I know, this is the most exciting project for my generation. With artificial intelligence, we will be able to calculate the dimensions of the universe and navigate its unfathomable regions with the next-generation robots we will create. Investigating the universe will be the point of harmony between humanity and artificial intelligence. For some, this means dehumanising man and opening up a new field in which we will find ourselves displaced or even undermined. But we are forgetting something fundamental; we are the only species on the planet that has understood that everything it sees outside the Earth is not a set piece, it is not a reality irrelevant to us. We have understood that such grandeur exists because it harbours infinite forms of new life, and it is in our power to be pioneers not only in discovering it but also in understanding it. Until recently, we could not even take flight. We have quickly taken to sailing the skies and going out into outer space, but we have soon discovered how fleeting we are in time and how limited our capacity for direct action is. Everything is thousands and millions of light years away and our lives only last for a short time.

'But just as we have realised that we could run faster with the train and the car than with our legs, and fly higher and faster with the airplane than any bird, so now are we just a step away from crossing the new frontier by creating entities that will enable us to enter the universe. How many new things we are yet to discover, and how wonderful the life of mankind can be if, using its intelligence, it becomes a civilisation focused on knowing and creating! And here, artificial intelligence can bring us a great deal—and if it does, human beings will love it. It is passionate work!' she concluded, her eyes filled with emotion.

'You could not have expressed better what is at stake and the greatness that awaits us,' Aziz told her, 'and it pains me that I cannot live long enough to see what I sense will be marvellous. The wise men preceding me always calculated to begin to map the universe, but they could not imagine that, once the map had been drawn, it could be directly explored by mankind. Do you realise, Nour, that a new sublime phase, unimaginable until recently, is about to begin? Man will pass from being *Homo sapiens* to being *Homo universalis*...'

And then they both winked at each other to celebrate their shared understanding and toasted with a few drinks of raki, a liquor that, according to tradition, leads directly from enthusiasm to nirvana.

The next day, Nour woke up full of energy. There was so much to do in this world despite the small bump in the road that the pandemic had brought, and her generation was prepared like no other to lead the way!

She packed her suitcase and, after breakfasting on some almonds with nuts and the traditional ginger tea, she said an emotional goodbye to Aziz, grateful for his wisdom and feeling that she might never see him again. She left for the airport with a certain nostalgia in her heart. Soon, however, she was on the plane to Istanbul, the city that had sheltered the wisdom of the West for so many centuries and had welcomed the subtlest of the modern Islamic world, and her mood changed. Istanbul's strong personality pulled her like a powerful magnet, and she was excited at the thought of being able to return to the city. Knowledge and refinement had always coexisted in this beautiful enclave uniting the origins of Asia and Europe, and Nour was aware of their virtues.

She disembarked at Istanbul's new airport, which had opened just a few months before the start of the great pandemic. Though it was now undoubtedly the largest in Europe, its internal appearance was bleak. It was immense, but empty. Designed to receive about two thousand flights a day, it was now receiving scarcely a few dozen. During the worst of the general lockdown, there were not even ten. The shops were mostly closed, and their footsteps echoed in the great corridors, but otherwise everything was easy. The entry formalities took her only a couple of minutes. She soon took the taxi to the Pera Palace, her favourite hotel, built at the end of the nineteenth century to house the passengers of the Orient Express.

Now it had been completely renovated. She liked to stay there because it bore the traces of a civilisation that was gradually fading with modernity.

She had arranged to meet Murat, a young researcher from her graduating class, who had returned to Istanbul after completing his studies in Hamburg. She was in close contact with him as he was always involved in unusual projects. Just before the pandemic, he had written to Nour, begging her to visit so that he could update her on all the interesting developments he had in the pipeline. She had initially refused, but, as the tide had turned, she told him that she would be able to visit at the end of her trip to Uzbekistan. He had responded enthusiastically, telling her that any date she could set would work for him. So, a few days before leaving Samarkand, she called him and they arranged to meet. When she landed, she sent him a message, and when she arrived at the Pera Palace, Murat was already waiting for her in the lobby.

'I'm so glad you made the effort to come in these difficult times,' he said as he greeted her.

'Yes, it really is all very depressing, but I couldn't help it. There's something about Istanbul that always brings me luck and, in addition, your enthusiasm and ability to tackle new subjects deserves all my admiration,' she said with a broad smile.

'Well, well,' he went on, 'so as not to disappoint you, I have prepared two things which I thought you would love. First, we shall see the dance of the dervishes, the great Sufi mystic rite, and then we shall dine on the edge of the Bosphorus, by the ever-so-slightly choppy, chalky waters of the strait.'

'I would like nothing better than to be able to hear about your ideas in peace and quiet, and the Bosporus at night offers us an unbeatable setting,' she replied. She went upstairs for a moment, put on an evening dress, and came downstairs quickly so as not to keep him waiting.

With hardly any traffic, Istanbul was a wonderful city. It was as beautiful and subtle as ever, but now everything was easy to look at, without noise, traffic jams, or anxiety. They arrived at the former great cistern of the city, which had been transformed into a peculiar theatre for the dervish dance performance. They settled down and soon, eighteen dervishes came out, spinning harmoniously on their own axis to the beat of music that methodically repeated the same musical phrases with the same rhythm. The conjunction of music and dance, the beautiful visual play of the tunics opening and intertwining as the dervishes whirled, created a sensation of time standing still that was hypnotic and meditative. It was a delightful hour in which the mind entered a higher stage of stillness. At the end of the show, Murat and Nour headed for the Bosphorus and, after crossing to the Asian shore, entered the Balaki restaurant, whose terrace overlooking the sea was one of the most coveted in Istanbul.

'It's good to be here, Murat,' Nour said once they were seated at a front-row table from which she could hear the lapping of the water. 'This city certainly has a special vibe. It was everything in the past. First, the capital of the Eastern Roman Empire, and then the capital of the largest modern Islamic empire. It is a meeting and flash point between the Cartesian world of the Christian West and the alluring and refined world of the Muslim East. And today, it continues to reinvent itself, with full energy and strength.'

'I'm glad you feel that way, because I'm passionate about it, too,' he said with sincere enthusiasm. 'It's a luxury to talk to you here about my current research.'

'Go ahead, I'm anxious to hear,' Nour said to reassure him.

'You see, today you have seen how powerful the Sufi dance and its accompanying music is, haven't you?'

'Yes, indeed,' she said, 'it has hypnotised me by transporting me back in time.'

'Exactly, exactly,' he continued. 'Along the same lines, I am using algorithms to research the impact of sounds on areas of our mind. I'm making progress in unravelling the relationship between sounds and mental states. And this can affect key aspects of our behaviour and activity. I'm building an algorithm to select the best sounds to sleep to, based on the rhythms, character, and several variables of each person. This is a field of experimentation beginning to be known as white noise. I analyse whether the sound of fine rain leads to deep sleep or, on the contrary, if the sound of a torrential but continuous rain is more effective. In relation to sleep, the key is monotony, and that's why sounds end up being even more powerful than music. It's a huge field to experiment with!'

'Absolutely,' she said, 'because till now man has been aware of the capacity of music and its effect on mood or ambition, but musicians have created it for aesthetic purposes and in an intuitive way. I try to go further. I seek to explore new capabilities of humanity through artificial intelligence by analysing millions of combinations between sound and brain. The mental resources that sounds can touch are enormous, and until now we have had limited means. I am diving into new waters, and yours seems to me a fabulous field of experimentation. I congratulate you and, above all, I encourage you to continue,' Nour said.

'Thank you,' he replied, his voice cracking with emotion, 'I'm very encouraged that someone as brilliant as you believes that this field can help transform the capabilities of human beings and their behaviour. Before you arrived, I was studying several cases of airplane hijackers, more than two hundred in the last thirty years, to analyse what kind of sounds could have neutralised them. I'm cross-referencing thousands of pieces of data. It would be wonderful if we could stop violent behaviours with the subtle management of sounds.'

Nour found the subject exciting, both because it was a virgin territory and was a field full of possibilities. 'A real field in which our generation can advance,' she repeated every time Murat outlined a new aspect of the subject and she, who had already accepted it, let her eyes wander freely over the black, sandy waters of the Bosphorus. They talked on until it was late. When fatigue began to overcome their will, Murat called the water taxi to take them back to the other side and accompanied Nour to her hotel. She dozed as they sped across town, and he woke her up when they reached the Pera Palace.

'I'll pick you up at noon tomorrow,' he said, 'so you can get a good night's rest.'

'I'm sorry I'm so exhausted, but it's been a busy day,' she replied before giving him an affectionate kiss as he opened the car door to let her out of the car and into the hotel.

For two days, Nour and Murat worked side by side to establish the research outlines he had drawn up for her on their first night. They made a lot of progress and experimented thoroughly. Nour worked at ease under that halo of passion for intensity. Istanbul stimulated her curiosity and pushed her to look for more and more. And by mixing sounds and human reactions, she was increasingly impressed by sound's influence on the brain. Strident sounds quickly triggered fury, disgust, and violence. Low, soft sounds aroused the imagination and could unsettle with an aura of mystery, and so on and so forth. What was new was that the sounds they could create had multiplied with technology, and their impact on the brain was also more detectable with the new artificial intelligence systems. There was an open field to invent new sounds and to register their impact on behaviour and memory and, consequently, on the actions of human beings. It was an immense field in which the new generation could advance and innovate without limits.

Nour's stay in Istanbul was brief. She had to take a direct flight from Istanbul to Athens on Saturday without postponing her departure. She said goodbye to Murat early in the morning with a very pleasant breakfast at the Galata Tower, watching Istanbul's hustle and bustle from one of its most emblematic places. From there, they could see the whole of the Golden Horn and how the big ships began to head for the Black Sea after hours of waiting at the mouth of the strait. Then they walked down the narrow streets leading to the bridge that connects to the modern part of the city, where the car was waiting to take her to the airport. 'We need you for the revolution in artificial intelligence we've been talking about. Don't stop giving me ideas,' Murat told her as she settled into the car.

It didn't take her long to arrive and get through all the formalities without any difficulty. The large airport was still operating at a minimum, and she boarded the Turkish Air Lines plane that would take her to the Greek capital in the blink of an eye with just a few fellow passengers. Waiting for her there was one of her best friends, Petros Andropoulos, a brilliant and innovative professor of educational science, whom she had met at many conferences. He had written to her insistently at the beginning of the pandemic to update her on his research into a new direction for education systems, asking her to spend a few days with him at his house by the Acropolis. She loved going to Athens, for the cradle of Western thought and philosophy filled her with vitality and an eagerness to learn. In addition, it was a pleasure to lose herself in the narrow streets full of taverns in the old town and to see the sirtaki, her favourite folk dance. She was also fond of Petros, a man much older than she was, but with an exultant vitality marked by an attitude that was always a little provocative, but full of generosity.

That seemed to be a common characteristic among many Greeks, but in Petros it stood out all the more, thanks to his innate tendency towards excess.

In his writings, Petros had made it clear to her how outdated the education systems were, and how they were wasting a golden opportunity for millions of young people who were not receiving what they needed to successfully enter professional life despite years of schooling. In his view, there was an enormous waste of energy and time. The curricula were outdated and did not take into account the extent to which the new generation was willing to prepare itself. Their positive will was wasted when students were forced to master subjects they did not need through obsolete learning methods. He was researching, through complex algorithms, how to redirect the processes and how to match what could be taught with what needed to be learned, considering the interests, skills, and personality of the student. In his informative missives to her, he always reiterated that nothing would help him more than to share his research with her, and that his house in Athens was open and at her disposal whenever she was able to travel. The subject had aroused Nour's interest and, now that the measures of lockdown had been relaxed, she had contacted him to meet in the Greek capital.

With the usual Greek expressiveness, Petros welcomed her with open arms. He took her suitcase, walked quickly in front of her to let her into the chauffeured car he'd hired, and began to talk without letting her take a breath. He wanted to fill her in on everything right away, although she kept telling him that they had time and that she would not leave before they had discussed everything. Right now she wanted him to show off the wonder of Athens to her because the lockdown had been so long that she needed to return to the greatness of humanity before touching the future. She needed to reaffirm herself of all that existed today before planning for tomorrow. And for her, Athens was a great zenith of the past.

They reached the old district and the car drove up to Petros' house. His terrace gave an incredible view of the Theatre of Dionysus, the largest of its time, situated a few metres below the Parthenon, in the middle of the Acropolis.

He showed Nour to her room, kept her luggage, and poured her a glass of chilled white wine to celebrate her arrival. They settled comfortably on the terrace and, seeing in Nour's eyes her admiration for the historic amphitheatre, he said: 'Tomorrow they open the season for the first time after the pandemic. It's a performance of Schönberg's *Moses and Aaron,* and you'll see how well we can follow the opera from here. The sound will be clear, and we'll be able to follow the scenes perfectly with our binoculars.' Petros liked the music, but above all he liked to show that he had one of the best houses in the city.

It was now noon, and they went out for lunch at a nearby tavern. It was in a small side street and had delicious calamari. The tables were made of wide, solid wood, which, being set a little ways apart, gave privacy.

'Well,' Nour said to Petros, 'now we can get to the point. I'm all ears. You can explain everything in detail and at length. With these views of the Parthenon, all my senses are listening!' And they both laughed for a while.

'You see,' he said, 'you know that in this land we are always asking ourselves how to further knowledge. Today, a fundamental question is how to train new generation in the face of the exponential growth of what we know and the multiplication of activities and new specialisations. Only if we manage to channel their will to learn towards clear results will we make rapid progress, and only then will they feel satisfied and fulfilled. But we must not forget that the new generations do not know how to train themselves, because this task is not theirs. They are at the beginning of the journey and they need to have the circuit designed for them. It is up to us, the generation that has already gained experience, to make the right curricula for them. If we design it badly, we will unnecessarily waste their energy and their chances of success. If we design it well, we will soon have great new professionals who will drive our societies forward and give the best service in their specialisations. We will have young people full of enthusiasm and energy, and the chances will increase that they will help improve the systems of study for subsequent generations. Success leads to satisfaction and a willingness to share. Tortuous progress creates frustration and resentment. It is vital to rethink education systems as it is the key to progress and the solution to providing for the high costs that advanced societies face due to longer life expectancy. Only generations that are more competitive, because they are educated more effectively, can contribute enough to support the older population. The surplus that they generate will be fundamental to support a growing number of retired people with increasing life expectancy. I want to concentrate on balancing the relationship between four crucial variables—each person's abilities, the field of knowledge in which they can best operate, what is known in that area, and how to pass it on effectively and efficiently. The aim is to ensure that no one wastes energy uselessly by being forced to take in unnecessary knowledge or to use inappropriate methods. The new generations are willing to study differently, but those who design curricula and educational content are reluctant to innovate; they only make changes based on obsolete models that they are reluctant to abandon. I need your help to calculate all this using in-depth knowledge programs. We should give numerous examples of how an educational process will lead to different outcomes with enormous consequences for both individuals and society. I have started working with several examples in the medical field which make it easier to understand the change that needs to be made,' he continued. 'Today, for example, the best bowel surgeon would be reluctant to operate on the eye, the ear, or the heart; either he could not do it or would not be sure if he could do it well, and he would delegate it to a specialist. If a widely renowned surgeon with perhaps thirty years' experience does not dare to deviate from his exact specialisation, why are we not training the new generations in a specialised way from the outset? Why do we not give them a year of general medical education and then devote the following years to a specialisation, to turn them into effective specialists of a precise body part in a short time? Then we would have great professionals in four years, whereas with the present system it takes perhaps ten or twelve years to reach the same position...that is if they get there and don't get demoralised along the way. Nowadays, a medical student, after six years of study, does not see himself capable of facing even the smallest operation on his own. Is this not a resounding failure of the system? We are at a time of great knowledge, and our challenge is for each individual to be a very intelligent actor in society. And we will only achieve this by helping each individual to discover their potential and identifying how to convert knowledge into something they can use in their designated field. By redirecting the transmission of knowledge appropriately, each person will absorb exactly what they need and each teacher will focus on how to deliver it.

'Wow, you're taking on a lot this time, Petros,' said Nour, 'but it's true that the field is exciting and requires so much work that we'll need to organise several teams to make it a success.'

'Yes, it's obviously a subject for the new generation to get involved in, and seeing how valuable time is—since a few months of paralysis have generated unemployment and frustration—you are entitled to demand that not a single minute of training days be wasted,' he concluded in a triumphant and impassioned tone.

'You're right, we can make great strides in better organising education through artificial intelligence,' Nour replied. 'With data we can accurately know what each person needs, how they can absorb it better, and what exact knowledge to transfer to them. I think this is a great field you're entering. And it also seems that the great pandemic can give a strong impetus to your approach, not only in terms of higher education, but at all levels of the long educational cycle. If, in the end, there is a period of limited face-to-face classes, all education will have to be virtual. If this happens, the model of a teacher with a disciplined class will come to an end. And to make the students, whatever their age and level of education, follow the virtual courses, these courses will have to provide knowledge that captures their interest. This opens up a whole era of content adjustment and a much more personalised organisation of knowledge. We are at the very beginning of the great change that may come, and your research is very timely. Do you realise how much the world will change if we move in this direction?' Nour asked. 'This artisanal world that has given us light will soon give way to a near-perfect world, with a spread of education never seen before. In a population of more than seven billion people, less than 30 per cent have clean water, but more than 70 per cent have mobile phones. This reveals how quickly we have implemented the technological revolution and how tortuous the industrial revolution was at the time. Today, the world is close to being fully connected and almost all individuals have the means to receive knowledge and information. Everything is ready for the new leap, the one you suggest, the moulting of the educational processes. The winds are favourable for transmitting knowledge in a much more precise and personalised way.'

'I'm glad that we are on the same page and that you're so clear about the importance of the transformation of educational methods by introducing precision factors developed with artificial intelligence. My only concern is the gulf it could create between the people of yesterday and the people of the future. Will the new generations be respectful of the previous ones, which they will soon judge to be obsolete?' Petros wondered aloud.

'It is true that time does not stand still, that every advance closes an epoch and opens the door to new attitudes as well as new problems,' replied Nour. 'Therefore, it is true that, if we move in the direction you say, it will accelerate the pace of life. We will become more efficient and the aspirations and habits of many will change with that, but we cannot give up the idea that everyone should be an engine of initiative. And by adjusting our educational systems to offer each student what they really need, we will give every member of humanity a chance at success.'

The next morning, Nour accompanied Petros to his university office. Classes had not yet resumed, and the campus was deserted. Only a few professors were in their offices. The emptiness was rather disheartening. However, it was not a bad circumstance for research. Day-to-day obligations had been reduced and it was easier to concentrate on the essentials.

He pulled out the pile of charts and documents on which he had been collecting his thoughts, and Nour was even more impressed by the enormous task in which he was immersed.

'I congratulate you,' Nour told him, 'I think you're looking at an essential topic to help the new generations make their study truly productive. When things return to normal, we will convene a special congress on this subject.'

'It will be fantastic,' he said, 'and by then I will have

a series of well-developed cases which will be eye-opening for a lot of people. And now that I have been able to update you and I can count on you in the future, we can go home and prepare for the marvel we will see this afternoon,' he said, picking up the scattered papers and putting his office back in order.

That evening they watched Arnold Schönberg's opera in the Dionysius Theatre, spellbound, from the balcony of Petros' house. It was a magical spectacle, and Schönberg's dodecaphonic music sounded even more mysterious and imposing in the great amphitheatre. At the end of each scene, Petros would give her a quick introduction to the next one as he had read about it extensively. It was a privilege for Nour to see it on that incomparable stage, and when it was over, she thanked him heartily.

'I'm glad you liked it. The theme was a premonition of your next wanderings in the Mediterranean waters. For, if Aaron was Moses' negotiator with the Pharaoh for the departure of the people of Israel from Egypt, I have been your special envoy to the captain of the freighter that will carry you from Athens to Algiers. I have arranged for you to embark tomorrow on the *Simeon III*, which is carrying cargo to Algiers, and which will enable you to cross the Mediterranean in three days. Or, wasn't this what you wanted?' he said with a knowing wink and a triumphant ironic tone.

'It's perfect. It couldn't be better,' she said, before

giving him an affectionate kiss.

They had a few glasses of wine to end the evening, and after chatting about the opera for a while, she went to bed. The day had been intense and exhausting. She was also excited by the idea of crossing the Mediterranean from cast to west. She wanted to imagine it while resting. She went to bed and began to carefully study the map of the route, the main places where the cargo would be delivered, and a little more about the history of the region, but her efforts were short lived. Soon her eyes closed, and she fell into a deep sleep. Once again, she found herself enthusiastically following the great debate about the construction of the new world.

Chapter 12

Giving Entry To The Power of Art

THE MAN with the capacity to bring forth the noblest contributions of humanity from the depths of the soul stood up. 'Yes,' he began, 'it has been said that people like me are the mediums who come to give visible form to the depth and content of the human soul. We bring to the surface what seems unfathomable. This is what Bach did, modulating sounds until they were encapsulated in unparalleled music that allows us to explore the infinity of the universe with our minds. We have been called artists, but I prefer to call us the revealers of intensity. Because all our work in music, painting, sculpture, film, and writing consists, has consisted, and will consist of capturing in external forms the most profound of humanity's innermost being. And, in the end, our work is what survives of the long journey of human beings through the world.

'In short, art elevates us above any other species because with it we can synthesise the spirit in words, articulate the intangible in the magic of the notes, and capture in forms and colours the visualisation of the energy of the era. Art is the only thing that remains.

'What else remains but the incomparable sculptures of Praxiteles, the fabulous work of Homer, the peerless temple of the Parthenon, and the written wisdom of Socrates? And what do we remember of great Rome? The great mosaics of Pompeii, the harmonious sculptures of Lysippus, the mighty Colosseum? What has been the legacy of five thousand years of the great Egyptian civilisation? Unquestionably, the beauty of the great giants of Abu Simbel, the chrome of Tutankhamun's sarcophagus, the colours of the frescoes in the tombs of the Valley of the Kings, and the imposing architecture of the pyramids. I could go on in the succession of civilisations in history, from Mesopotamia to the Incas, or from the Western Middle Ages to the golden age of the Eastern empires, or the prodigies of contemporary times.

'And today, I am thrilled to be able to speak here in the Hall of Human Rights and the Alliance of Civilisations, where one of the great artists of our century has bequeathed to humanity a great treasure of contemporary art. It shows how art overcomes the artificial frontiers that we have erected to manage life in society. I am struck by the fact that art today dominates our debates. This omnipresent dome, with its grandeur, its forms, its colours and its intense vitality, which Miquel Barceló has painted here for humanity, is a symbol of the central place that art should have in the life of the planet. The United Nations was right to integrate art into the central room of its debates and negotiations.

'It was remarkable that the first place where Art, in capital letters, was incorporated was in the room where the Human Rights Council meets. It is a sign of great hope for all—hope for the significance of the new body that has been created, the greatest advance of this organisation in this century, and for the organisation's awareness of art. This encourages me to convey what the art world has asked me to add to the debate of this hearing convened to shape the world of the future.

'Today, fortunately, the world of art knows no frontiers. Music, painting, photography, architecture, writing, dance, or film, whatever is new, magnificent, or masterful penetrates every corner like unstoppable wind. But, the important thing is that in all genres and mediums there is no single line, no school, no central axis which limits; rather freedom and creativity are the only basic rules that should govern this activity of humankind. Diversity is no longer an affront, a challenge to be controlled; it is the lifeblood that sustains art, just as it sustains life itself. And we artists are thrilled to witness the creative process of those who have something great to show. All of us, whether we come from Africa, Asia, Europe, or America, are united by expectation. We all come to see what will appear, not who has produced it. And although its creator is important, when what is produced is marvellous, it takes on a life of its own and becomes everyone's property. So it is with the frescoes of Romanesque art, concerts of Baroque music, or the caryatids that support the Parthenon.

'The artists want you to do the same with the government of the world. What really matters is to provide us with a common building where all human beings can create, whatever their ability, origin or territory. Let their relationship be with a unique space that allows them to create and reach their full potential as spiritual beings. The important thing is that rivers of innovation flow into the sea of humanity.

'Today, we artists like to link our work to the human soul rather than to a limited reality. We want people to be connected by the power of sharing projects and discovering new possibilities, not by the geographical mark of their birth. Modern art freed painters from having to reproduce people, objects, or places and allowed them to explore pure painting. Similarly, human beings must be able to focus their activity on developing their potential as human beings, without being constrained by the narrow limits of a specific spatial organisation.

'As has been said before, it is good that we have moved from tiny territorial organisations, the tribes; to more medium-sized ones, the small kingdoms; then to larger ones, the nations; and finally to the very large ones, the federations of states. This is all well and good and shows that we are travelling in the right direction, but I would ask you now to speed up the pace to reach our final destination, the completed space—the world. Getting there will enable us to focus on what is truly important to each and every one of us—to live our existence to the fullest and create.

'We are beings with a limited, but unique, moment in time to create and explore the capacity to live. Creativity is the sign of our identity as a species. Our short lifespan is our Achilles' heel, the evidence of our fragility. Let us remove everything that stands in our way and hinders us in this process, for our greatest mistake is to waste the little time we have been given, without discovering, knowing, and enjoying how much we have at our fingertips, for this planet is a marvellous reality.

'As an artist, I could not agree more with the statement bequeathed to us by one of the world's great explorers, the Norwegian Thor Heyerdahl, when he said, "Frontiers? I have never seen any, but I have heard that they exist in the minds of some people." Please, let us not fragment a world that has been given to us without limits and let us heed a cry that is already beginning to take shape. Let us organise ourselves so that we are no longer limited by structures that dwarf our existence and lead to confrontation. We need a new world to progress safely, and I trust that we will know how to empower ourselves with the necessary greatness to do so. May the extraordinary character of this hearing, the strength and beauty of the art that presides over it, and the enlightened recommendations that are being put forward, inspire us and lead us to forge a different future. Nothing could be better than for the new charter of the world political order, of which the Secretary-General has spoken, to be like a multi-coloured fresco which would embrace diversity and establish the new human identity. Each human life could then develop as a work of art, with the whole of humanity reaching a higher stage.'

And, lowering his tone in his last words, he raised his eyes to the dome, towards its great fiery red centre, symbolic of the strength of the spirit. Everyone instinctively looked up at the great work of art, and spontaneously applauded.

Chapter 13

Towards Algiers And Dakar, Across The Sahara

The desert and the sea: New agriculture and new energy
Entering the era of virtual museums

AS PETROS had announced, Nour left Athens for Algiers on the cargo *Simeon III.* Now she had time to sail to Algiers. She was in no hurry, so she need not fly. She was going to spend three days crossing the Mediterranean, one of the most beautiful seas on the planet, observing in detail every kilometre of its coastline. What a pleasure and what a privilege! Her most beloved book was the *Odyssey*, and destiny smiled upon her by allowing her to sail through the blue waters of the Aegean. What a marvellous way to reach Algiers, sailing the entire length of that sea where the great civilisations of the past had been born and often collided. How many times in the past had Persia crossed that sea to invade Greece, Rome, or Egypt? Today, the two shores were very different—in the south, the relative standstill of Arab civilisations lost in the labyrinth of modernity and, in the north, the progressively ageing European populations living in beautiful cities. She decided to begin her journey by returning to read Homer's *Odyssey* again, the book which teaches the virtue of being imaginative in life. In the afternoon, while she was rereading the chapter on the farewell to Circe, the ship passed the great white cliffs of Zakynthos on the way up to Corfu, and from there passed the Straits of Messina, trusting that Scylla and Charybdis would be asleep by this time. With her great tonnage, the ship moved steadily forward, without rocking, and this gave her great security.

The next day they skirted the dry and rugged coast of Libya and stopped in Malta in the afternoon. Nour took the opportunity to walk for a few hours and marvel at the historic centre of the island. A refuge of the Templars and a central base in all the wars, it had distinguished itself as the only place in the wide arc of the European Mediterranean that had never fallen into the hands of Nazism or fascism—an incredible feat in the face of the ferocious Goliaths! Then they would cross the beautiful bay of Carthage and finally reach Algiers. Saltpetre, and at times an intense smell of iodine, accompanied her during the whole voyage, and none of the hours were heavy or monotonous. Such is the charm of the seas.

As she neared Algiers, her excitement grew. At last, she was going to do something that had always attracted her and which she never expected—travelling down through the desert to Dakar. Her friend Abdelkader, with whom she had been living for three years in Hamburg, had kept telling her about it when they were a couple. 'It's the most beautiful and intense thing you can do in this life,' he told her again and again. They lived together for three beautiful years. He was an inconsistent artist, but sometimes he produced quality canvases. In the end, he was asked to direct the new museum of contemporary art in Algiers, and he accepted. Their lives then went their separate ways, but they had maintained a good relationship.

Now the pandemic had changed everything, she thought of taking advantage of the invite that Abdelkader had always extended to her. She called him and heard the enthusiasm in his voice. 'Of course, Nour! I'll organise it, and I'll go with you. The museum will still be closed for a few days, and we'll have a good time. What's more, I have an important appointment in Dakar, so I'll be able to keep my word,' he said before hanging up.

The *Simeon III* docked shortly after dawn. Abdel was waiting for her in the port, chatting with one of the fishermen who came day after day without fail to catch small fish, more for pleasure than for earning a few dinars. It was the beginning of summer and the heat forced people to fish early. She was very happy to see him. He was still as slender and handsome as ever. His angular face, his long, strong arms, his green eyes, and his direct and warm gaze made him a very attractive man. Besides, he had character, personality. Though fate had led them down different paths, nothing had quite died between them. 'I'm so glad you've come,' he said, taking her hand as soon as she got off the boat before giving her a big hug, 'I'll finally be able to show you my country, and show you that everything I told you about the desert is true!'

They went to breakfast at a small café just outside the port. Most of the big restaurants in the city were still closed according to the official order, but some small ones took the risk and stayed open to survive by any means necessary.

They had some delicious sardines, and then a Turkish coffee that delighted Nour. 'Ah, this really reminds me of the coffees I drank when I was young in Damascus,' she exclaimed, before tossing back her hair as she let her mind wander a little to childhood memories.

They paid the bill and got into the jeep. 'I have everything ready,' he said proudly. 'It will be a long trip, a once-in-a-lifetime experience, but you'll like it, you'll see, and above all, you'll be impressed by it.'

They crossed Algiers to take the desert road leading to Tassili. The city was a desolate sight, with no people on the streets and hardly any cars on the main road. Who would have thought that this paralysis, which was driving everyone towards nothingness, would be possible! But they soon left that devastating and sad picture behind them and entered the torrid desert. 'It will take us two days to reach the Tassili plateau,' Abdelkader told her.

'We're going to take a long detour on the way to Dakar, but that will give you a unique experience. Although going along the coast of Morocco is much quicker and easier, I want you to have this desert immersion experience, so we will take the old caravan route, down through the Sahara and into Dakar from Mali. This way we'll be going over a thousand kilometres through the heart of the desert, but what you'll discover at the end will fascinate you.'

After nine hours on the road it got dark and Abdel stopped the vehicle next to some high dunes well sheltered from the wind. There he set up the small tent he was carrying in the car, prepared a fire to roast the lamb he had included in the provisions, and boiled water to make tea.

That night they told each other about the thousand things that had happened to them since he left to settle in Algiers. They finished the lamb and were enraptured by the utter silence of the desert.

The sky was clear, full of stars, and the small fire, nestled between large stones to last all night, crackled and threw small orange-red flames that ended in hundreds of golden sparks. It was a beautiful moment, and they could not contain the passion that attracted their lips together. They were long kisses in a night that was all for them. They began to kiss each other slowly, sensually, with exquisite pleasure, enjoying every moment, and ending up carried away by passion.

'You know,' she said, 'there's no one who kisses as well

as you do. You know how to take us straight to the paradise of desire with your kisses. Pleasure runs through your lips, caressing that delicious state of pleasure that exists in love.'

'Thank you,' he answered and, looking intensely into her eyes, he said, 'Under the immensity of this starry sky, where the slightest sigh interrupts an immense silence, everything becomes more magical. We have the whole night before us to fall into the depths of love so that we may enjoy the overflowing magic of Eros.'

They entered the tent, and the light of the fire outlined their two slender naked bodies to perfection. She put her arms around him and felt the strength of one who has all the muscles carved like an Apollo. And he was sweet and strong, provocative and suggestive, loving and determined. And, after making love to the quiet rhythm of the night in the desert, both fell asleep with their bodies intertwined until the first rays of the sun announced the arrival of day. It did not take them long to gather everything and resume the journey to the Tassili.

They were again long hours on the road. The sun reflected off the road, creating a misty mirage in the heat, and in the early afternoon they reached the village from which you climb to the plateau of Tassili. There Sifaw, a young Tuareg, was waiting to show them the way and to give them new provisions. After a while, they began the walk up to the magical place that keeps the most antique engravings of humanity. Those big rocks perched on the arid plateau, like old menhirs exhausted by the sun and wind but surviving upright and dignified, kept inside them the most amazing engravings of antiquity—huge men up to six meters high, massive heads with some shades of colour, and fish that crisscrossed at their feet, painted thousands of years ago.

Nour could not restrain herself from caressing those impressive paintings.

'What a marvel!' she said, 'what a treasure!

'Yes,' said Abdel, 'it is perhaps the oldest museum of humanity.'

'How did they ever think of painting these fish?' she asked him.

He smiled, for now he could explain to her the significance of the region in the world thousands of years ago.

'They painted fish because a great river flowed through here, which some say was the continuation of the Amazon, back when Africa and America were united. And the amazing thing is that even then the inhabitants of these lands mastered the techniques of pigmentation as some of their colours have survived to this day. The art is the only thing that survives.'

When the sun began to set, Abdel set up the tent in a large hollow between the rocks and prepared a small fire to roast the peppers, aubergines, and pumpkins that Sifaw had given them, which he would mix with yoghurt and paprika for dinner. He also set out the bread and almonds he had brought with him. They ate quietly, savouring the freshness of the crusty bread and the taste of those fresh vegetables that in the desert were a gift from the gods.

'These paintings are a mystery,' she said as she brought him the mint tea.

'It is true that the size of the painted humanoids is a great mystery. The huge heads, the tubes coming out of the top, the enormous bodies. Who was here thousands of years ago? One thinks that history is linear but perhaps it is not, and is instead punctuated by special chapters. For example, contact with beings from elsewhere that certain cultures may have been privileged to have. Perhaps this was one of them,' he said, a little shaken. They were both silent for a while, as if turning over their thoughts, spellbound by the crackling of the fire. At last, it was Nour who articulated her thoughts:

'It is exciting,' she said, 'what you have told me, that there used to be a great river here, and that hundreds of different fish had their paradise here. Today, this could also be an orchard,' she said in a low tone, as if throwing a stone at a calm pond. The night invited her to be daring.

'The sea, after all, is not so far away, and today it is feasible to desalinate the water and use it for irrigation. The technology has advanced; the cost has only gone down, and even more so here, because solar energy could be used. Pumping it through the desert would not be difficult. It's all very flat. And with your country's richness in phosphates for fertilisers, the land could be fertile in a short time. This could be a thriving country in the new agriculture,' she said.

'It's all right in theory, but I don't think anyone would have the courage to get involved in something so bold,' he replied.

'Why not?' Nour persisted. 'Today we are studying how to set up a first colony on Mars. There's no water there, no atmosphere, no air, everything from start to finish must be artificial. And yet no one involved in the project thinks it's unrealistic. Here, on the contrary, everything is within reach. The water is nearby, we just need to desalinate it. We have land in colossal proportions, and we only need to fertilise it. We have plenty of sun and air at no cost. Obviously, we have to organise it and work hard, but it is by no means an impossible undertaking.'

'You don't know how hard it is to work here from May to October, when the sun melts even the stones,' he said, trying to close the subject.

'We have to think differently, Abdu,' she said affectionately. 'First, we have to consider that we could put the hardest work in the hands of robots.

'As everything would be created from scratch, we could prepare for the reconversion of large tracts of desert into new large agricultural fields, so that most of the operations would be done by autonomous tractors and the farmers would take care of the operations of programming the different machines using artificial intelligence systems. We could also think of new, intelligently-designed villages that would create a comfortable life for the new inhabitants. A growing humanity must have access to new possibilities. Do you think there is overpopulation? No, not at all. There is over-concentration in certain small areas that host cities, but look at the thousands and thousands of miles that are completely empty here! Then they say that there is a lack of food and that we will not be able to feed an ever-growing human population. And, I say that it is foolish to think so. What is happening is that we don't know how to make the most of the immense empty spaces on the planet, like this one. We don't know how to organise ourselves efficiently, how to attract new settlers, and manage the political implications of this new reality. It is all a problem of not knowing how to operate with criteria for the future. We cannot be victims of a surmountable impossibility. And, all this would be possible with artificial intelligence systems. There could be a comprehensive operation to transform the desert into a great agricultural reserve.'

'I have always admired your enthusiasm and your forceful strength,' he said, touching her gently, 'but this time you have surpassed yourself. You pose a colossal challenge, a titanic task.'

'You're right, Abdu,' Nour replied, 'but what I'm telling you can change the future of your country and can give new horizons to many people. And I believe that our generation can do it. Our generation cannot be swallowed up by the renunciation of everything, as some people fear will happen with this pandemic. It is a generation that has to take action, and demand that the few means at its disposal be used to open up new horizons, not to distribute charity. The Arab world created the most admirable orchards of its time and became the most advanced civilisation in science before the West took over. Why should it not be able to rise again and regain its strength with artificial intelligence, setting a new course for the future? It is possible, and it is up to the bravest to try.'

'I hope you're right,' he said, his fingers caressing the cup of mint tea that was still warm. Then he picked up the light blanket he had brought, went over to Nour, wrapped it around her tenderly, and said in her ear, 'You have spoken like the great teacher everyone recognises; let me now reward you by making love to you like a little servant,' and he stroked her neck as he led her into the tent he had carefully prepared for her to enjoy that night to the fullest.

He had put jasmine scents in the oil lamps that hung from the tall poles of the tent. The flickering of their flames cast suggestive shadows on all the walls and tinged the atmosphere with a warm yellow. The scent of jasmine was strong and intoxicating. On the floor were rough Berber kilims and on these the thick sheepskins that made it soft.

He carried her inside eagerly and, once inside the tent, began to undress her with care.

'I don't want you to be in a hurry today. We're in the place where art began in the world, and I want to go over every corner of your body, first with my fingers and then with my lips, so that the memory will be indelible when you leave a few days from now.'

Then he slid his fingers, covered with spice oils, all over her body, letting their aromas arouse her and provoking an intense desire in her.

'Feel free to enjoy yourself as much as you want, for only the stars will be able to hear you tonight,' he said before powerfully wrapping his arms around her to begin the rite of love, feeling deeply every part of her body.

The next day, they descended from the rocks of the Tassili and continued the journey by jeep into the heart of Mali to reach Dakar.

'We'll stop for a few days in Bamako,' he told her as they headed down the long dirt road through the desert. 'I've contacted the director of the museum of African art, Adib Al Ahmi, an interesting man, Dogon, very capable and active, with whom I get on well at cultural meetings in the French-speaking world. I have been promising him for some time that I would visit his museum, but I have not yet found the time. He also has a daughter who is becoming a promising photographer and wants to show me her work to get my opinion.'

'That's fine with me,' said Nour, 'I'm sure it will be interesting.'

They arrived before sunset in Bamako and went directly to Al Ahmi's house on the outskirts of the city, where most of the Dogon people lived. The house was large and overlooked the great desert plain that lies south of Bamako.

Al Ahmi welcomed them with the traditional hospitality of the Dogon, the most aristocratic tribe in central Africa. In their tradition when someone important arrived, they dined in the large inner courtyard with the whole family and their closest friends. With this welcome, they want to show that they are honoured by the visit and that they want to share the best they have with the guest. There were dates, almonds, and crusty bread on the table, along with two large platters with the two lambs that had been roasting all day, drizzled with honey and covered with rosemary. The conversation was lively but formal, respecting a hierarchy that only they knew. When night fell, Al Ahmi asked his daughter Amina to come over, bringing the albums where she had collected her photos of the desert. With great respect and classic Dogon dignity, she approached on her father's right side and placed two large albums on the table. Amina was beautiful and slender with a look somewhere between feline and sweet. Feline because of the strength of her jet-black eyes that silently scrutinised everything, and sweet because of her warmth. Al Ahmi made room for her to spread out the albums. She did so, and soon there were sounds of great admiration. Most of the photos were in sepia and showed the unique Dogon in their life in the desert. They were unique documents, taken by someone who had captured the soul of this mythical tribe. Abdelkader ran his hand over some of the photos as if to verify that those people were not alive on the page, but were virtual faces, such was the strength of many of those photos. 'I congratulate you,' Abdel said to Amina, 'you've done a great job. Africa needs to present itself strongly in the world of photography. So far, this form of art has been dominated by Westerners and Asians. The Westerners for the themes and the Asians for the perfection of technique. You are breaking new ground with the intensity of life in your shots. I like your work,' he said sincerely. Her eyes sparkled and she sensed that her future could change.

The next morning, they were awakened at the dawn by the thunderous sound of all the animals. Nature was on the move with the sun, and it was impossible not to follow it. After having breakfast with the Dogon's traditional drink, the jinibré, they returned with Amina to look at the albums of her work in detail.

'I could take them with me to Dakar,' Abdelkader said. 'They want me to be the curator of the next Biennial of African Art and I could start talking to them about your work.'

'Yes, of course, take them,' she said. 'It would be great if they liked my work!' And she ran off to her room and returned with a set of somewhat damaged photos. 'These are from when I was just starting out,' she said with some excitement. 'Perhaps you might also like them for their simplicity.'

That was the key word in Amina's work. Simplicity as a synonym for authenticity. It was like taking the camera to the very human soul of the ancient people who looked the viewer right in the eyes, who were not afraid of anything. It was the conjunction of humanity with nature. It was a beautiful revelation in these times when recovering the soul of the planet required so much energy.

'I like them,' he said again, after looking at each one carefully. 'I'll take them, too. I think that'll be enough to convince them.'

After breakfast, Nour and Abdelkader continued their journey to Dakar. The farewell from Al Ahmi and his family was very warm. They were showered with all kinds of gifts and loaded with provisions for the journey. Al Ahmi gave Abdel a big handshake as a sign of deep gratitude:

'Thank you for coming and for taking the trouble to spread Amina's work. She will have a long way to go, but you will have opened the way for her. Our hearts will not forget,' he said in a deep, serene voice.

They soon left Bamako behind and were lost in the horizon on an endless, straight road flanked by the desert under a fiery sun.

'Seeing these immense empty, flat, open spaces, along with the power of the sun,' said Nour, starting the conversation anew, 'one can't help but think of the possibility of transforming these spaces into the planet's new solar energy reservoir. Thirty years ago, it was hard to imagine what to do in this vast desert. Today, on the other hand, it seems impossible not to sense that it will soon be one of the richest places in the world, producing millions of kilowatts of energy. What great transformations await us!'

And for hours, alone in that ocean of dryness, the two of them unravelled the immense possibilities offered by emerging technologies in the future transformation of the desert.

'It will be a mechanical world that will be built here,' said Nour in conclusion, 'and again there will be a great paradox—the most scorched and, therefore, abandoned space on the planet, will produce the energy that will feed us all. From nothing will come everything. It may well be a new economic dawn for the continent.'

'I knew you would be impressed by the desert and that it would make you see things differently,' he said, 'but I didn't think you would go so far in seeing so many possible transformations. I am glad that so many days under this fiery sun have not been a nightmare but rather the beginning of new thoughts for you.

'And when we get to Dakar,' he concluded, 'you will

be immersed in a new field in which you will also be able to contribute a lot. This time it will not be linked to the desert but rather to the long history of negritude.'

She then asked him to continue so that she could prepare herself a little.

'You see,' he said, 'Gorée is the little island opposite Dakar, and on it, for four hundred years, slave traders organised a great flow of slave trade from Africa to America. Some eleven million slaves captured in the interior of the continent were locked up in different enclosures on the island, which today are called slave houses, to be shipped from there to the new continent. At the tip of the island there is a fort that changed owners, sometimes belonging to the English and at other times to the French, and from there they fended off pirate attacks. The island was, thanks to its security, a key bastion in the slave trade between the West and the New World. Recently, an important international figure proposed to the mayor of Gorée that a museum with virtual contents be established there.

'The idea was to create a new generation of museums organised with only virtual content to revisit the island's past and build on the successes of negritude in the world. The idea gradually made its way into the mayor's mind. He finally discussed it with the Minister of Culture, who has been mulling it over. I met the minister at the last meeting of senior cultural leaders of the Francophonie, and a few months ago he called me to ask my opinion.

I told him at the time that I thought the proposal was innovative, and that I would like to discuss it at the build site to better visualise the project. When you called me, I contacted him to see if the dates worked out and, when he confirmed it, I was able to set Dakar and Gorée as our final destination. He asked me to think about this proposal in depth and I took some ideas with me.'

'Interesting,' she said, 'keep going.'

'The spread of culture is going to change radically with the digital revolution,' he added. 'Young people today are highly interactive, communicating all day long through social networks. In Africa, this trend is even greater than elsewhere as they have gone from rural to technological in the blink of an eye. In Africa, young people are the bulk of the population, and the virtual is ideal for attracting the younger generation to the temples of culture that are museums. This museum in Gorée could be the beginning of a new conception of museums throughout Africa.'

'Very interesting,' she said again. 'I'm interested to know more.'

'This museum could have two floors under the ground, emerging at the surface halfway up the third floor, from where you could see the sea. It would be like seeing the horizon of freedom. On the lower floor, the visitor would experience the most outstanding moments of the development of Africa through virtual techniques.

'The most important episodes in the history of Africa

could be relived virtually—the tribal world, colonial spread, cultural transformation. It would be a floor dedicated to the roots of the continent's identity. The next floor would house three hundred figures of people who have contributed the most in the long march of negritude towards freedom. From slavery to freedom, what a hard road! Each figure would have a human face that, when touched, would briefly explain its role in history, and a video would be projected with the historical moment of the character. Through these three hundred personal journeys, we would learn a lot about the evolution of the African world, and we would be able to experience their emotions, hopes, doubts, and sufferings directly. It would be a floor dedicated to the roots of freedom. And then, in an adjoining room, visitors could identify their personal roots, following the path of their family tree. This would add a personal component. Lastly, the upper floor would house the triumphs of blackness. And the triumphs are many, in culture, politics, economy, science, sport, music, painting, photography, so on and so forth. In it would be the men and women who have put a face to these high points, these great contributions to human civilisation. We would call it the roots of glory, and that is why it would be the top floor, where you could see the sea and the African continent.

'I see it,' he continued, 'as a unique museum with great appeal to the world because of its two great virtues.

First, it would offer the public a crucial new experience, and secondly, unlike the enormous investments that are required today to create a traditional museum, this one would be low-cost, so that it could be replicated on other topics in other parts of the world.

'The project would be a cultural appeal from Africa to the world. I find this project fascinating because of its great potential and its novelty.'

'Right. And you know what?' Nour suggested, fully committed to the idea. 'You could add one more dimension to it that you might not have thought of yet. And I'll tell it to you to complete your presentation. Through artificial intelligence programs you could create personal museum tour circuits. Instead of being a linear visit, the same for everyone, the visit could be organised for each visitor in a personal way. The visitor, on arrival, would express his or her preferences and an artificial intelligence program would contain an algorithm that, combining the visitor's personality and interests, would organise the best sequence of the visit to the different rooms of the museum, so that each visitor would have a personal experience. The system would suggest, for example, touching the faces of totems 5, 80, 150, and 238, which would be the most striking for them. In this way, artificial intelligence could turn the visitor into an even more active subject in the museum visit by making them a protagonist. Each visitor would be a unique actor and the emotional dimension of the experience would be heightened. Upon leaving, each visitor would have the impression of having experienced something very personal. A subjective visit as opposed to a traditional, passive one.'

'Brilliant, I think it's brilliant what you've said, Nour, and it certainly widens the gap between the museum of yesterday and the museum of tomorrow. And, in contrast to the high cost of classical art museums borne by some emerging countries, this one would be a revelation, and the poorest continent of the planet would become the epicentre of innovation. A deep shiver of excitement runs through me just thinking about it.'

And he gave her an affectionate kiss after stopping the jeep for a moment beside the sandy track on one of those long straight sections that seemed infinite, only interrupted by the rolling terrain.

After more than a thousand kilometres of arid road, they finally arrived in Dakar. They rested that night in a small hotel by the sea, and the next day, at noon, they went over to Gorée. The mayor and the Minister of Culture were already waiting for them at the small pier on the island.

'Welcome,' they said as Nour and Abdelkader jumped onto the pontoon.

'We are honoured that you were able to come at this difficult time,' the Minister of Culture told Abdel.

'What's promised is what's due,' he replied matter-offactly, 'and besides, I was able to travel with one who is a prominent figure in matters of the future, the researcher in artificial intelligence systems, Nour Aswan,' he said, looking at her to introduce her.

'It's a pleasure,' said the minister and the mayor. 'You are very welcome on Gorée.'

The four of them advanced quickly to the fort that was a few metres from the pier, on the far-right side of the island facing west. There, the municipal technicians and several public figures from the world of culture were waiting for them. They sat down in the main hall and the mayor explained the project of the new museums of Gorée. There would be two, one dedicated exclusively to the difficult history of slavery and the march to freedom, and the other to the future of Africa. The first would be housed in the fort they were in, and the other, a completely new museum designed by a group of prestigious architects, would be located on the slope of the small mountain.

The presentation was clear and precise, and began a wide-ranging debate among those present. Abdel did not rush. It was important that everyone speak and feel that they were the protagonists, and so he should keep a certain distance. On one hand, he was the foreigner and, on the other, he was considered an authority on museums in Africa. It was better to maintain this aura with measured silences and active participation in the conclusions. The project was now a little different from what he had explained to Nour during the trip; there were not one but two museums, but it had taken a turn for the better. It would make Gorée an example in Africa, not only for its past but also for its capacity for innovation with a constant circulation of initiatives for the future. After several hours of debate, a clear consensus was forged in favour of starting the work soon. During the concluding session, the minister proposed that Abdelkader should lead the project. It seemed important to him that the museum should be borne with a global calling for Africa instead of being limited only to one country, so putting it in the hands of a man who had not been born there, but who had accredited prestige, seemed ideal. He also believed that the future component of the project, to be the most advanced virtual museum in the world, seemed the best bet, and Abdelkader was known for his knowledge on the subject. The proposal was accepted, and the minister gave him the floor to say a few words.

Abdel began by saying how exciting the challenge was. He saw it as the new door opened in Africa to culture,

'The virtual world is part of the lives of young people, and Gorée's virtual museums will be the most innovative, drawing a crowd first from Africa and then from everywhere in the world,' he began.

He then explained how he would integrate many disciplines, from history to politics to art, so that visitors would be immersed in the complexity of the history and could experience strong feelings. He concluded by explaining Nour's presence at the meeting and asked the minister to give her the floor. The minister approved immediately. Nour did not want to elaborate too much at the end of the meeting, but she outlined the possibility of incorporating artificial intelligence systems into the management of museums in order to personalise the experiences of each visitor, as she had explained to Abdel during the trip.

At the end, she concluded by saying, 'I congratulate you, and am pleased that you have decided to promote these projects. They will be born under the sign of the dynamism and constant renovation of their contents, which will make them a centre of creativity of the first order in Africa. Gorée has a deep sense of soul; as soon as you approach it, you perceive its unique energy, and walking along its streets you can feel it with intensity. It seems amazing to me that you endow it with this dimension of the future. It will undoubtedly be a success and an example for many other places.'

That night the two of them slept in one of the old slave houses. Abdel had expressly asked the mayor, who gave orders to prepare the one closest to the sea. They had spent almost ten days together crossing the Sahel, but destiny would separate them again the next day. Finishing the trip in Gorée seemed to Nour to be the perfect end to those intense days. The next morning, they woke up to the sun streaming imperiously through the open windows. They had slept through the night completely intertwined, as if trying to defend themselves from the immediate sale of their bodies.

For a few moments, the fear of the slave penetrated them, and they huddled together waiting for the fatal moment of separation. It would come, but it would be less tragic. Nour would continue her long journey, while Abdel would stay a few more days in Dakar, making progress on cultural projects, including Amina's exhibition. They made love for the last time. Nour boarded the first boat of the morning to head back to the mainland, and from there took the direct flight to London as the city had just reopened its airport. Two hours later, she was inside the British Airways plane that would take her directly to the English capital.

She settled comfortably in her seat, drank the glass of white wine offered to her and, shortly after take-off, fell asleep peacefully. In her sleep, she again landed in the great hall of the Palais des Nations.

Chapter 14

The Architect's Hour

THE MAN who wanted to adjust the world by combining every new building harmoniously with nature took the floor. He rose in earnest, climbed gracefully to the rostrum, and spoke with the assurance of someone who is half artist, half scientist.

'I have come to speak to you,' he began, 'about what could be a life of quality for all humanity, for it is up to humankind to add beauty or destruction by transforming the appearance of the planet with their projects, plus the capacity to distribute the population well or badly over it.

'We are the only species that can erect buildings taller than the flight of a few birds, create cities that are as large as great inland lakes, and connect populations with prodigious bridges and tunnels. As beings that transform the space that nature has given us, we cannot continue with the same methods in the future as we have done in the past. Let us look at where we are and where we come from.

We are on a beautiful planet, and we come from beautiful nature. We stand as intelligent beings and that means that we must add intelligent things to nature. Everything we build is meant to stay, to endure. We cannot add anything repugnant. Our duty as an intelligent species is to know how to improve what we have received.

'Great works are the most transcendent of humankind's deeds. They bestow the greatest dignity on the history of humanity by fixing all its greatness in an enduring way. Don't our eyes water with emotion when we contemplate the temples of Angkor in Siem Reap, the Valley of the Kings in Luxor, the pyramids of Giza, the Arch of Hadrian in Jerash, and the wisdom of Rome in preserving buildings from many different centuries in the same space? In these constructions we imbue the soul of man in different times, because, by inhabiting them, we have left our mark on the interior and by erecting them, we have permanently embodied our dreams and aspirations. Space transforms man, and man in turn transforms space. That is why this dimension of human action should be given special consideration in this noble assembly.

'Today, with the wisdom that we are accumulating in our civilisation, we have to set new horizons in order to know how to plan any new construction in the future. Only if we organise urban planning and architecture well, can we lay the foundations of a quality human life and make our transformation of nature acceptable. The work of man will be a work that exalts the beauty of the planet.

'In the relationship between what we build, our lives, and the planet, there are three main issues—how to build in a way that every new space enhances human life; how to build so that the artificial fits well with the natural; and how to distribute the population and the buildings more harmoniously on the planet.

'The reason why I am talking to you about this is because we must be concerned about promoting the quality of life globally. For we should prevent the beauty in the progress of some places from being spoiled by the ugliness that takes over others, or the wisdom of certain regions promoting small, well-articulated cities from being spoiled by the unordered overcrowding elsewhere. If we really want to protect the world, how man inhabits it becomes a global question. This highlights the importance of conducting our development as a global species, not fragmented by borders and artificial divisions.

'As I was saying, space transforms man. There are many essays and works on how people's behaviour and moods change depending on the spaces that enclose them. Houses, factories, theatres and hospitals all have an impact on what happens inside them. The time has come to make buildings intelligent and more human.

'On the other hand, humankind transforms nature with its constructions and modulates space in its own way. Once, a highly respected architect told me a maxim that has guided my work ever since: "Good town planning saves a bad building, but a good building without good town planning collapses." And I would add, without urban planning, without adding pieces to a harmonious whole, no matter where it is located, city, town or open country, everything loses its value.

'Nature works with specific numbers to grow in harmony, numbers discovered by the Italian mathematician Fibonacci progress with the sum of the previous one, going from one to two, from two to three, from three to five, from five to eight, eight to thirteen, then twenty-one and so forth, allowing this series to proceed.

'This allows us to observe harmony in the development of the roots of the trees, the leaves of the plants or the petals of the flowers, in whatever the forest or jungle we visit. Humankind must assume that in the future everything must advance under the conception of harmony of the whole. There are many cultures and many ways of building and enriching ourselves with different conceptions, but all of them must delve into their rules of harmonious growth in order to enhance their particular contribution. And once this has been achieved, we must enhance the value of the pieces. We must make each new construction stand out like a sculpture because of its beauty. My words may seem difficult to live up to in the poorest areas, but I want them to receive these words in a new light and to remember that they are the result of a long life of work on the five continents. Everything is more contingent on the attitude than on the means. In my travels around the world, I have seen the most beautiful small buildings in the poorest places. A tiny, well-finished window, a well-placed timber in adobe walls, a well-carved wooden door, all make for an endearing dwelling, full of human warmth. At other times, on the other hand, a large building made of expensive materials but with poorly calculated proportions and miscalculated colours and shapes stands out as an eyesore in a city. It is therefore appropriate to think of every new building as a new work of art, whether it is a great skyscraper, a humble building, a new generation of museums, or a large factory. In this way, we will strengthen the positive character of humanity and add a new dimension to the world.

'We will add yet another beauty to nature in addition to the many that it shows us. We will have understood its fundamental law—harmony.

'And finally, here is my third point. At this time when we are coming together to better organise our future, we cannot give up the idea of pioneering a new human settlement in the vastness of the planet's space. Many have spoken of overpopulation, and I would like to tell them that this is a mirage. What exists now are small areas where we concentrate large populations. These are the great megalopolises that swallow up millions of people, but, however large they may be, they are just a drop in the bucket compared to the total space of the planet. When we take off from the great metropolises like New York, Shanghai, Mexico, Buenos Aires, São Paulo, Bombay, London, Paris or Moscow, don't we see them disappear in a few minutes and soon find ourselves faced with huge empty spaces? The challenge is not overpopulation, but the proper distribution of humanity in the vastness of the planet's space.

'And now that we are gradually overcoming the great constraint of having to be close to each other to work, it is the right time for innovation in this field. In the beginning, it was important for people to be close together to defend themselves and generate knowledge. This is how the first cities were born in all cultures. Who is not fascinated to discover the charms of Fez, Florence, Bruges, Samarkand, or Xi'an, with their narrow streets that exude human closeness? But today, the new world of interconnectedness has led us to overcome this need, and as the digital and virtual are gaining importance, we can dissociate between where we live and where we work.

'So why should the immense plains of Central Asia, the vast expanses in the heart of Russia, the immense deserts of Africa and the Middle East, or the whole of the interior of Latin America, where it is sometimes difficult to find a human being, remain empty? The great technological progress we have achieved allows us today to reformulate our relationship with space as sedentary beings. And if we used to prosper by huddling together in cities, today we can aspire to a new model. It is time to move to provide quality of life for humanity. Let us aspire to live in houses that stand like works of art amidst vast expanses of nature. Many will be able to enjoy living in pleasant places while working at a distance, such as the doctor who performs a surgical operation five thousand kilometres away, or the engineer who directs a construction site on another continent in real time. New technologies allow us to separate action and space, and this is a great revolution that should make it easier for us to change how we settle on the planet.

'The One Humanity world can unlock talent everywhere, and that talent needs to manifest itself in the seminal area of architecture. The world is transforming every day with the emergence of new constructions. Today the challenge is to operate under a new pattern—the mandate of harmony, whose father is urbanism and mother is the wise hand of the architect who understands the insertion of the individual in the whole.

'Do not think that what has been said is of minor importance or that it is only applicable in a limited way. No, every corner of the world deserves good urban planning and good architecture.

'The world will see how their lives will change if they live and sleep under a shelter that inspires them and fills them with satisfaction. And humanity will flourish in splendour if it spreads out without bottlenecks and wisely accommodates itself to the possibilities offered by the vastness of the planet. Achieving this will be the most beautiful proof that humanity has entered a new era.'

Having said this, he sat down, letting the weight of his words sink into the audience, and giving way to the next speaker.

Chapter 15

Towards London

The transformation in medicine and the time limit of life

NOUR ARRIVED in London just after dark. From Heathrow, she took a taxi to The Berkeley Hotel, in the heart of Knightsbridge. She liked the Mayfair district better because of its proximity to the art galleries, which in London immediately connects you with the latest trends. That night, however, her friend Jessica, who had been so insistent that she return to London, had recommended that she stay at the Berkeley because she had arranged their dinner with three eminent doctors. As the taxi drew nearer to the centre of London, a sense of familiarity came over her. That city had the best dimension of any she knew, in that it integrated diversity like no other, and decade after decade, it was always in the vanguard. Neither ostentatious nor superfluous, it distilled the essentials of life and valued irony and humour. That is why it was difficult for a worthwhile idea or a promising initiative not to fall into the right place and quickly take flight there. There was an exquisite wisdom in how to ask questions without wounding or wasting time. This was a city that knew how to preserve the essence of the flavour of things and, without wishing to be invasive, it was extremely incisive in knowledge. It was also a city that was difficult to master and demanded effort to learn its many secrets.

It takes time to get to know it, but the reward is to get fascinated by its intrinsic greatness. Its strength lay in the richness of its diversity. At first, diversity is disorienting, it escapes easy references that define a closed world and requires a great openness of mind and attitude. With time, one eventually discovers that the taste for diversity is, in itself, the identity of the city and that which unites it most is seeking out what creates surprise.

In recent years, she had travelled extensively to London. The major universities were vying for her to give lectures in postgraduate courses that advanced the study of deep knowledge and artificial intelligence.

She had nearly arrived at the hotel, already enjoying the colour of the London night. The faint yellow of the streetlights made the cityscape very warm, very human. Then there was that combination of short houses with an infinite number of shops that filled everything with life, although at that moment the usual bustle was missing because of the pandemic. The cab headed down Brompton Road and soon reached its destination. She was fascinated by the way London cabbies always managed to get to their destination without any questions and by the quickest route. She had never seen better professionals in the world than London taxi drivers, and when she researched its reason, she found the explanation in the exam they had to pass to get their license. The English had turned that industry into a highly professional one to the great benefit of those who used it. 'What intelligence in the organisation of a collective service,' she said to herself.

She entered the hotel and noticed that everything was marked by a certain sadness, nothing shone like it did before. With the devastating wave of the coronavirus, the hotels had suffered colossal losses and service had been decimated. Those that were open were operating on a shoestring. The Berkeley had all the usual charm inside, but it lacked the joy of yesteryear, the fruit of opulence. Everything was now very spartan. She was assigned one of the rooms overlooking Knightsbridge. After a quick shower, she went down to the bar to wait for Jessica and the group of doctors. She asked for a cosmopolitan at the bar. The lounge was completely empty, but it was still extraordinarily beautiful with its art deco chairs and clear ceramic lamps. This was the place she liked best in the hotel. Jessica soon arrived with neurosurgeon Elias Patten, cardiologist Lawrence Scott, and epidemiologist James Cohen. They were all in their forties or fifties and at the height of their popularity.

Jessica made the introductions and they immediately moved into the private dining room prepared for them. It was a minimalist style dining room with harsh tones, decorated with paintings of American neorealism that gave it a sense of elegance. The cardiologist Lawrence Scott began the conversation by thanking Nour for her visit:

'We are very interested in meeting you,' he began, 'because the three of us, in our fields, are doing in-depth research into the replacement of vital organs with mechanical instruments. We wanted to learn more about the research you are involved in to create replicants endowed with artificial intelligence and similar capacities to human beings.

'We began replacing elements of the body with mechanical parts a few decades ago. Until then we had been replacing certain human organs, such as the heart or kidneys, with similar organs from other animals, but a few years ago we incorporated mechanical valves into heart operations. And today, we are well on our way in the design of fully mechanical hearts to replace the fleshy ones we are born with. And we are doing the same thing with nerve endings, the liver, the lungs, the eyes and, of course, the bones. Our only barrier at the moment is the brain. We are impressed to learn that the artificial intelligence entities that are being created have the ability to self-regenerate when they fail. They can fix themselves and repair a broken arm or an eye that does not focus properly.

We are interested in knowing what their limits are.'

'The truth is that we are advancing very fast and we don't know how far we will go in our investigations,' Nour replied. 'We ourselves are amazed at how quickly we improve all the artificial intelligence systems we create, and every day we add young researchers full of ideas who open up new lines of advancement. The ability to identify a fault or problem and regenerate is at the core of every new creature we give birth to. In humans, pain gives us the signal, but it is true that we lack direct regeneration. We need you doctors!' she said with a note of humour.

'There is one area where artificial intelligence could change the lives of many human beings and enjoy the highest prestige, compensating for intellectual disabilities,' said Elias Patten, the great neurosurgeon. 'So far, for us, people with intellectual disabilities are beings that we care for but consider less capable than those who are not mentally handicapped. But the latest studies show us that, because of their peculiarities, they have developed powerful functions in areas of perception that the rest of us barely exercise. Artificial intelligence can help us to understand the characteristics of their brains, and by finding compensatory mechanisms in the areas of deficiency, enhance their superior abilities in other areas that have gone unnoticed until now. Human nature sometimes gives some people this compensatory factor directly. I remember a deaf man who became one of the best perfumers in the world because he developed an impressive olfactory ability and maximum concentration in the study of smells. With new algorithms, we could process a lot of scattered data from the actions of the disabled and better understand their uniqueness. Here artificial intelligence will play a key role as a social integrator. It will help effectively integrate the diversity of those with an initial intellectual disability.

'On the other hand,' he continued, 'the big debate is when do we stop being who we are through mechanical substitutions of our organs? If we can begin to replace everything, even the circuits in our brains, can we continue to be who we are through mechanical replacements of our organs?

'Will we continue to be ourselves or will we become home to other consciousnesses in our original body?'

'You've touched on two very important issues,' Nour replied. 'Today, we are at the dawn of an unprecedented revolution in medicine, and you are the ones who know the most about it. Operations can be done remotely, certain organs can be made with 3D printers in remote places, tissue regeneration by inserting cellular molecules will completely stop ageing, and the development of new artificial organs will be accelerated. This raises questions about the limits of existence and what constitutes the essence of every human being. All of us researchers who focus on the development of deep knowledge systems are asking ourselves these questions in depth. I must admit that we are at the very beginning of everything, and our greatest achievement is to bring together interdisciplinary groups of philosophers, doctors and engineers who suggest data and variables from different angles to extract new orientations. But an immense field is opening up, a task for a whole generation. With each new medical discovery, a new opportunity opens up to insert artificial intelligence into its development and, with each advance in the understanding of human nature, we can better build the robots of the future efficiently.'

'Listening to you makes my mind go in so many directions at once,' said Jessica. 'To think that in perhaps fifty years' time, men and women may live much longer than a century, thanks to the constant regeneration of their whole composition, from the most physical parts of the body to the brain as a whole, is beyond me. And, if we are going to get into speculation, we can go even further, will death exist in the future?

'Today, births all over the world are constantly decreasing. Each individual begins to consider its own existence as the only thing that matters. If we accept regeneration, there will be those who will soon put all their efforts into extending their lives exponentially in the hope that the next stage will be to overcome death.'

'That will not happen in this generation, but I will not deny that it may be a reality at the end of the century,' said Nour. Softening the gravity of her words, she added,

'There is still a lot of research to be done before we can glimpse that horizon with any certainty.'

A deep silence fell over them all. They hadn't intended to reach this point when they started dinner, but the exploration of new capabilities in medicine, combined with the application of artificial intelligence systems to drive their new breakthroughs, had led them to see the new world very clearly.

They ended the dinner talking about the hot topic of the moment, the great pandemic, and James Cohen put it in perspective:

'Life is full of diseases that resist control, from cancer to malaria to AIDS, and we can't rule out that this virus is here to stay. If it resists eradication for a while, we should focus on controlling it within acceptable limits. What do you think, Nour?' he asked, trying to lighten the mood again.

'The effective response to this pandemic virus will undoubtedly come from medicine, but today the two fundamental variables, when and how, still seem uncertain,' Nour replied. 'Research is being done along the lines of a hypothetical vaccine, but experts do not know whether or not we can be immunised for a reasonable period of time. It seems that the body's memory is short against this infection and this, if confirmed, would greatly jeopardise the effectiveness of any future vaccine. On the other hand, we are working hard on the development of antivirals that slow down or hibernate the infection, as was done with AIDS. We want to see immediate results even though it has taken us almost twenty years to stop AIDS, and neither have we been able to find a solution for other viruses such as herpes or the common cold. Nevertheless, the world's investment in supporting medical research to curb COVID is colossal and will undoubtedly yield faster results. Hopefully, the research will soon lead to success, but in the meantime, it is certain that we can do a great deal in the organisational field to neutralise its spread. One promising field is group testing, and artificial intelligence can be of great help in selecting the population to be tracked. On the other hand, there is no longer any doubt about the value of new mobile tracking applications based on artificial intelligence algorithms.'

'Certainly, until we find the antidote, information is going to play a fundamental role. Only with artificial intelligence systems will we be able to quickly process all the new data and take operational containment measures with the least possible disruption,' said James Cohen. Looking admiringly at Nour, he concluded, 'Until medicine saves us, we will have to rely on the skills of people like you.'

They finished the dinner talking about how and where each one had spent the most difficult period of lockdown. Little by little, the amount of humour in these anecdotes grew as the night wore on, and dry martinis, at Lawrence Scott's request, made their appearance. After an intense debate, they needed to relax a little, and as the evening progressed, a synergy grew between them that would leave its mark and bring them together.

By the time Nour went up to her room it was late. She was exhausted, but satisfied that the meeting had been very enlightening. 'What interesting people,' she said to herself as she tidied up some notes she had taken. Fortunately, the next day she was taking the afternoon plane to New York and would be able to rest all morning. Hundreds of ideas were swirling around in her head about how humanity would change due to the exponential advancement of medicine. And she wondered what communication between generations would be like if life spanned many decades in each one. She smiled as she changed, as if finding a glimmer of ingenuity in the idea, threw herself on the bed, and fell asleep at once. Her dreams took her back to the great hall of the Palais des Nations where the debates were proceeding apace.

Chapter 16

The Entrepreneur's Hour

THE MAN who created the machines that transformed wind into energy, handmade products into millions of units, and metal into cars, boats, and airplanes took the floor. Slim, wiry, and with a serious air, he began a speech that vindicated the ability of entrepreneurs to drive humanity forward by transforming ideas into reality. 'In our efforts to transform ideas into reality,' he began, 'lies a large part of the progress of humanity. Our work is never without its dangers, for everything that is new is by definition unaware of the imponderables that will accompany it. But we dare, and where many theoreticians are afraid, we go forward. We are driven by a powerful energy to translate ideas into reality. And in doing so, we multiply work and wealth.

'Those who have spoken before me have set out in detail the magnitude of the challenges and threats we face, and they have done so from the broad perspective of their vantage points. I am in the engine room; I belong to those of us who make the world move every day by creating the products that reach millions of people. I would like to bring to your attention the tragedy that the standstill in business caused by the pandemic has wrought for all those who make a living from their work. The wheel of commerce has begun to seize up and employment has collapsed like a house of cards. And this affects the stability of many because employment underpins the dignity of the majority. The figures showing what it has meant to have the world in disarray for a few months are chilling. And the worst is yet to come because the states, having to sacrifice productivity, will begin to run out of income as they have paralyzed those who generated it. In a short time, a truth that some know, but many insist on ignoring, will be palpable, that only by generating wealth can the whole of a common building be sustained. But not every outlook is negative. I have also come to speak to you about how the economic activity of humanity can change, to ask you to understand the change of course and facilitate the transition, redirecting resources and opening the doors to those who promote the new paradigm. In this noble organisation that brings us together today, important work has already been done, first by approving the Sustainable Development Goals, and then the 2030 Agenda. There is an awareness that a major change in resource management must be undertaken and that the future must be different from the past, but I would like to emphasise on the economic change itself.

'Today, we are entering a new paradigm of economic and social life. We are moving towards a world in which each individual must become a precious piece of dynamism and initiative, and in which the public sector must be transformed so that it is first and foremost a contributor to economic and social dynamism of society itself.

'Never has so much knowledge been shared as during this unexpected lockdown, never has each person become so aware of the uniqueness of his or her life as during these months of forced isolation, and all of this is taking place in the fertile ground of limitless global communication. The physical closure has been accompanied by a prodigious opening of the mind, and this is the key to our future. The digital economy has received an enormous boost, with remote work taking root in a way that would have been unthinkable a few months ago. This is the direction we all knew we had to go in, but it is only when driven by the unfolding of events that we tend to get going, and this is what has happened once again. The pandemic has really given wings to the digital economy.

'With the rise of communications and the development of virtual reality, the world has been able to turn towards a new direction in which each individual takes on their full significance. It is no longer important for people to be a work force but rather to be a source of creation. The individual emerges as a great world unto themselves, as the key unit in all human development, and the age of the mass workforce may be coming to an end. Today, the great pandemic has turned this dynamic on its head as risk and fear of contagion deal a mortal blow to all that is collective and massive.

'It is a colossal paradigm shift, and we are at a crossroads that is both fascinating and extremely complex. The scenarios for the future are opening up, but we must redirect our investments to ensure that the tempo of change is successful.

'The existing revolution in the transmission of knowledge makes it possible to train millions of people using new methods. Everything is now possible and novel, and there is no other way out than to redesign activity. How to work, where to work, and what to work on in a world that will be more and more individualistic. It is a revolution that technology has initiated, but which the emergence of COVID is accelerating exponentially. And with it, human beings will become less and less a workforce and more and more the brains of initiative and invention, handing over mechanical functions to machines programmed by artificial intelligence systems.'

The depth of those words brought a great silence in the room. All the delegates had grasped the importance of what was at stake and were beginning to take an interest in the man's precise ideas.

'When we ask how to reorganise ourselves in order to preserve peace, and strengthen the positive dimension of humanity, we must emphasise that it is only through constant progress that we can aspire to be a civilisation of harmony and prosperity. To this end, it is essential to maintain a world in great activity, and what is now changing, since we cannot operate under the paradigm of mass society, is that we must base it entirely on the value of intelligence. A world focused on imagining and creating. A world essentially of entrepreneurs always connected virtually. By pushing us into isolation and distancing, the pandemic forces us to explore the intellectual capacities of each individual. Fortunately, it coincides with the moment when we have begun to interconnect.

'The pandemic will continue, and the contagions will become unstoppable, it will accelerate our entry into a new phase of development. Economic activity will be boosted in a new way. This is what I define as a new paradigm.

'Citizens must be determined to create. The wise men who came before us have all pointed to imagination as the special gift that has led humanity to distinguish itself from the rest of the animals and to set itself up as a singular and superior species. Imagination is our great gift, and the ability to bring our imagination to life is our great strength. I advocate for a humanity that imagines, for a species that distinguishes itself by making each member a mover of new realities. This will change the world and usher in a new era.

'In this order of things, an idea that must prevail clearly in everyone's mind is that we must move forward in generating even more wealth, so that there can be more research and new discoveries and so that we can quickly reach the other side of the shore, where the material is no longer a problem for humanity. Communication is spreading on a global scale and lockdown has solidified virtual communication. Language barriers will now be overcome through automatic translation by the devices so that everyone will be able to communicate. The essence of a thought will be even easier to transmit since the virtual is better able to withstand simultaneous translation than the physical. This will mark a twofold revolution in learning and in the speed of discovery.

'On the one hand, we are at the beginning of the unlimited capacity for virtual learning. Millions and millions of people now have the tools to receive information. We can acquire new capacities to act if virtual learning is well organised since digital channels enable us to overcome the limitations of traditional learning, which was restrictive by definition. Let us acknowledge that today the capacity to learn is multiplying exponentially.

'On the other hand, let's bear in mind that communication has historically been at the basis of all progress. Moving from villages to cities expanded the dimension of communication and the world began to multiply its discoveries. The light, the car, the airplane, telephones—machines of all kinds arrived. Moving from cities to the world as a single, fully connected space brings us into a new dimension in the capacity for invention, as the seed of ideas expands without limits. Great novelties are in the making!

'Let me give you two examples to show the magnitude of the transformation in progress,' he said with humility. He had gradually been gaining the appreciation of the large audience. A silence full of expectation fell in the room, so that no one missed the details of the man who spoke with the credentials of being in the workshop of the world and knowing the capacity of action of mankind.

'A century and a half ago,' he said slowly, 'we didn't have electricity or combustion engines. It was in 1881 that Edison produced the first incandescent lamp, and in 1860 that Étienne Lenoir made the first internal combustion engine.

Since then, the world has been filled with power plants and motor vehicles. Today, the planet is home to nearly two billion cars on the road. Do you realise how much change has been triggered in just a few generations? Well, it will be even greater because of the change driven by the generations that will follow. Electricity will be generated in many other ways and mobility will be mainly through the skies. The mastery of the sun's rays and wind power opens the door to a new conception of energy use and production. The advance of artificial intelligence opens the horizon to individual aviation, completely transforming mobility schemes.

'Yes, if the era of crowds and masses is coming to an end, mobility will have to be reinvented. It will be the beginning of the individual air age. Millions of drones will have to be developed as new transport vehicles which, following in the footsteps of starlings, can operate safely and autonomously in the skies. This will free us from the constraints and limitations of fixed and heavy infrastructures like those on the ground, giving us new horizons of freedom. The enormous costs that we will save on these fixed infrastructures can be diverted to the low-cost production of mobility units. Millions of aerial transport drones can be created now just as we created millions of cars in the last century. It will be up to us to develop new aerial legislation to facilitate their use, but there's no one better than this noble assembly to push it forward. The technology is there, since vertical take-off and landing drones are already in the pipeline, and we will have just to develop new aerial legislation to facilitate their use.

'They will be able to leave and arrive from anywhere, bypassing the dependency on airfields and airports. Let's keep in mind what is essential, mobility has to grow, not stop. Rethinking it in individual terms will be the solution, and that will only be possible through the skies where the routes are infinite, and the infrastructures needed are very few.

'So, we are entering a world of individuals and innovations. The first step has already been taken, individuals are becoming more aware of their uniqueness. Clearly, though tragically, this pandemic has consolidated the prominent position of the individual. We can learn and create many new things if we do not erect barriers to our common progress.

'Let us be convinced that at the crossroads at which we live, it is imperative to direct our energies towards better organising the world's economic future. But we cannot forget to carefully note an essential reality—our level of progress does not allow us to make mistakes without colossal costs for the well-being of all. And of all the possible mistakes, the most dangerous and deadly is war. At this point in history, it is impossible for mankind to enter into a war without completely destroying its well-being. That is why, Secretary-General, I cannot conclude without deeply thanking you for having put on the table the central issue for the future of humankind—building the new global political architecture is the top priority.

'We business people can do much to promote progress, but without a new global political architecture, peace and security, and therefore the future of all of us, will always hang in the balance. I would therefore like to express my confidence in the delegates present here today, confronting the challenge we have to face. The importance of what is at stake leads me to rename this assembly as "the assembly of hope for humankind", for it must lay the foundations for the progress of all.'

Letting this call to hope float away, he gathered up his papers, tucked away his glasses, and calmly descended from the rostrum to sit down in a discreet place in the room.

Chapter 17

To New York

Communication, a central element of the new era

NOUR WAS back in New York, a city emblematic for having been the world's gateway to modernity for many decades. Nevertheless, while that city continued to innovate constantly, other large cities now seemed to be moving faster. In New York, the weight of what had been created was beginning to have such critical mass, such a presence, that it was becoming the symbol of an era and, therefore, a city that counted as much for its past as for its present. It belonged to the category of those places with history that have taken on many layers of life. However, most importantly, it was a city that understood the commitment to artificial intelligence.

Nour loved its light. That wonderful light of May, above the great avenues that open out to the horizon, paints the sky with pastel blue, and a soft ochre tone slowly descends. It is a light that invites hope, decisiveness, and the start of promising projects.

This time she had booked her favourite hotel, at the end of 60th and Fifth Avenue. Since she stepped off the plane, thousands of memories of her previous stays kept flooding her mind. This time the big city had a calm pulse, for the pandemic had caused great depression and pain. Despair had taken hold of many, but she had no doubt that it would find a way to recover. Its entrepreneurial character played in its favour—it was in its DNA, as its supporters said. Decisions were made quickly and the dimension of the projects was always large. Nour loved that people were so diverse and showed so much initiative. She had some very bright friends there, and they were such a breeding ground for ideas!

That night she was having dinner at the home of friends who had a large apartment overlooking the East River. Kenneth and Ann Dangrave were two of the city's most famous architects. In Nour's honour, they had invited to dinner a group of friends linked to new media and finance who wanted to meet her: the president of a social networking giant, Bob Baltin; the head of the leading digital content multinational, Rose Hughes; the head of the largest audio-visual media group, Paul Hayser; and the financier Chris Barren.

Ann made the introductions, and the conversation became livelier as everyone arrived. They were in the living room next to the dining room, from which they had a wide view of the river. The sun was setting, and it was beautiful to see the skyscrapers on the opposite bank turning an orangey ochre and gradually maroon and silver as the sun went down. It was an urban landscape that exuded power. The conversation was fast-paced and to the point, and soon Ann invited them to sit down.

On the way to the dining room, Nour thanked her hosts for their kindness in hosting the dinner. Ever since they'd met at a conference on artificial intelligence and architecture held in New York five years ago, they had kept a close relationship.

At the conference, Kenneth had spoken about new designs in skyscrapers with the introduction of titanium and new glass that could be moulded into the boldest of shapes. Nour had talked about new technologies with remote programming, which make it possible to operate houses and all kinds of buildings in the absence of their inhabitants in a personalised way. Kenneth and Ann had been very interested in her applications, and she had teamed up with them to integrate the newest generation systems into their new projects.

As soon as dinner began, Ann openly posed the topic of conversation:

'What do you think is the most remarkable change that these turbulent times have brought about?'

It was Bob Baltin who began the debate:

'It is clear,' he said, 'that communication has become the winner. Human contact is suffering, but not so much communication. It is another type of relationship, and this opens the door to new types of behaviour and habits. It has been impressive how some communication platforms have multiplied their users exponentially. If one of them had managed to gather ten million subscribers in the last three years, today there are two hundred million, and perhaps by the end of the year they will reach three hundred. This means that the power of communication has grown exponentially. Without having to travel, everyone can be more focused on searching for information, tracking down what they need and making virtual contacts. Therefore, I believe that we are on our way towards a world more inclined to virtual communication.

'This will enhance everyone's ability to find the most diverse information and to seek answers to their unique questions online. The capacity to communicate through social networks and new technologies has multiplied at an accelerated rate. Many now have access to all kinds of discussions that they were previously completely unaware of. However, progress must be made in helping to use time in an operative way. The challenge is what is communicated. And, above all, how we manage to neutralise the intoxication of false news and close off the way to manipulation.'

'Yes,' said Nour, 'this really is a big issue, how to neutralise falsehood and manipulation in an age of open communication. There are rivers of information in which it is hard to tell who is launching or manufacturing the news. Evidently, it all begins with the awareness that not everything that is said or circulated is true, and nor is it presented without interests. But how can we know this? I believe that this opens up an enormous field for artificial intelligence programs capable of tracking fake news and providing data to focus more on facts than on interpretations. We must get into the habit of looking at the data and checking it, and we can do this by means of technological programs.'

'I totally agree,' interjected Rose Hughes, 'and may I congratulate you on your brilliance in explaining how to function in the new free world of communication without being dragged into censorship to avoid manipulation and mischief. Another world that is opening up is that of the new generation's fascination with virtual programs. In the solitude that we have entered into in the contemporary world, many found their pets to be a vital new companion early on. Along with the love of nature, there is also a certain splitting of personality that occurs when establishing a special communication with another being that seems to understand but replies little. I think this is now going to multiply in some people's relationship with machines. What do you think, Nour?'

'Well, obviously, the new artificial intelligence programs can create virtual beings that make great life companions,' Nour began. 'Just as we have developed sophisticated game programs in which a virtual being can be just as accurate as a flesh-and-blood player, chess being a clear case, we can delve into each person's personality, know their ambitions, fears, desires, and the behaviours they expect to encounter when communicating in order to develop their perfect partner. This field is certainly full of possibilities, and I don't think it is feasible to close it off. We must start integrating this facet as a new component that will be more and more present in societies. The problem is obviously the autism that this can lead to, but perhaps someone will also create programs to neutralise the isolation,' she said with an irony that hinted at the spiral of new applications that could soon burst forth.

'And, taken to the extreme, we'll fall in love with a virtual Character,' said Paul Hayser, reminding everyone of the plot of the movie *Her*.

'Certainly,' Nour picked up the subject, 'and that's starting to be a problem with the new generations, who are so familiar with all things virtual that they're beginning to prefer virtual sex,' she said. 'Virtual sex leads to more daring scenarios than are common in real life.'

Rose Hughes replied, 'We are putting a lot of money into programs that make it easier to find companions more quickly. With the ability to communicate, people's time has undergone a dimensional change. The patient searching, wandering, discovering, once essential components of life for making friends, activity-mates, or joining circles of people with common interests, is now becoming a clear source of frustration for those who want to maximise their hours. Many are beginning to find it more useful to express exactly what they want for a system to find the companions. It's getting straight to what you want and, although you lose the magic of the moment of discovery or encounter, you gain in richness of experience. It's another world, but I think that's the era we're entering.'

'I agree,' said Nour, 'and here too the key will be how to strengthen the accuracy of information and avoid deception and manipulation. And as this new way of relating to each other develops, we need to look at how it affects and changes behaviour. In this emerging new world, the new generation will have the opportunity to be highly creative and innovative.'

'Speaking of behaviours,' Bob Baltin interjected, 'I was recently told of a new application, still in the experimental stage, to identify the interests and motivations of any counterpart in any kind of conversation or negotiation. If it worked, it would have an enormous impact on human relations.'

'It is true,' said Nour, 'important advances are being made in this area. Today we deal with the limited mechanism of psychology and personal intuition. The most perceptive people pick up on each other's desires or interests earlier, but that is not the case for everyone. Just as simultaneous language translation and facial recognition programs have been developed, we are also on the verge of developing algorithms that, based on responses, intonations, looks, and gestures, will make it easier to understand what the other person is motivated by or looking for.'

'This would complete the communications revolution,' said Paul Hayser as they served the main course, meat with raisins and apples. 'In the twentieth century, we developed various devices and instruments to connect us—radio, cable telephone, television, computers, and the internet. In the twenty-first century, we have taken a giant leap forward with mobile phones and smart phones that connect us to each other anytime and anywhere, and allow us to operate in a multitude of fields. The software will soon follow that enables us to communicate with each other in a real and effective way: the development of instantaneous oral and written translation systems which overcome the language barrier and makes it possible for all human beings to understand each other. If a Brazilian and an Icelander were previously able to transmit their voices to each other from the opposite side of the world, now they can speak in their own language and the other can receive it in their own, making the content sound intelligible. And soon will come the program that will allow us to know everything about the nature of the relationship between ourselves and others, a program that, when linked to a search engine that can search anything about the other person that might interest us, will completely transform the way in which we progressively relate to each other.'

'It's exactly like that,' said Nour, 'a whole revolution that also feeds back on itself. The more you can do, the more you look for the mechanism to make it possible in a more immediate and accessible way to a greater number of people, and from that comes the appearance of a new invention that opens up yet another new horizon. Communication has expanded the power of humanity globally, a whole new perspective in our evolution.'

'In my field,' said financier Chris Bren, 'the changes are also set to be huge because of the impact of communications. In addition, as the replacement of cash by modern payment methods accelerates, transactions generate precious information about how people use their resourccs. This gives the people in the financial sector a much better understanding of the habits of millions and millions of people, which until recently were invisible due to the anonymity of physical money. This change is of great magnitude because companies that have the data will also break into the financial chess game, displacing traditional operators, who will suffer from the rigidity of their structures and a lack of information. Credit will become like a glove for applicants when it is administered by the new operators linked to huge databases as they will respond precisely to the wishes and possibilities of each individual. The same will be true of fundraising and in the attraction of saving. Not to mention the profound transformation in the means of payment.

'We all know how bitcoin has been gaining ground, but this virtual currency is just the tip of the iceberg of a great change. The pandemic has given a major boost to the digital economy, and new blockchain-like mechanisms will appear that will arbitrate exchanges more transparently. We are in a turbulent sea where the bold will take risks and we will see the entire fabric of financial agents transform.'

'And finally,' said Paul Hayser, looking at Nour, 'since we're privileged to have you with us today and to be able to put some very important issues on the table, how do you see the relationship between human intelligence and artificial intelligence? Do you think the systems we will create will surpass us?'

'Well,' she said, 'my colleagues and I are having serious discussions about this because it's a very open issue. The present is fundamental to the direction of the future, and how we oversee the constant advances in artificial intelligence will determine whether we can control its evolution. We must bear in mind that many artificial intelligence programs have the capacity to improve themselves based on their own functioning and, therefore, left entirely to their own devices, may end up initiating dynamics beyond our control. Thus, for example, in games the initial programs have been perfecting themselves and are now always victorious over human beings. Their capacity to advance and improve is exponential. What might happen if artificial intelligence systems one day want to rebel against humans? The most direct way would be interference in communication.

'Imagine that they are able to understand all the codes of communication. They would then be in a position to alter them. Let's imagine that they introduce dyslexia in air communications, or in the computers of autonomous vehicles and that, given a piece of information, for example that the position is 24/15, they intervene in the communication transmission process, and the other party hears 42/51, then the number of accidents would be enormous. All communication is codes, and artificial intelligence systems could hold a position of power by becoming skilled in interfering with the content of communications. It is therefore crucial to think about how to regulate the future development of artificial intelligence, just as the development of money led to the creation of central banks, or the development of communal living led to the creation of the police to ensure positive coexistence. Anarchy in this case is very dangerous, and our security depends on the creation of a supervisory body on a global scale.'

In a few words, Nour had put the focus on the centrality of communication in our advanced societies and on the need to know how to protect ourselves. The discussion then opened up, and they examined from different angles how to create this authority without it becoming the great power or having a hierarchical nature.

Then the desserts arrived, which Ann and Kenneth had taken special care to prepare, knowing that their friends liked them very much. Cake and ice cream of different flavours delighted everyone, and the hosts received very kind compliments.

The conversation took flight, and Nour's gaze escaped from time to time to rest on the magic of the East River, where the great skyscrapers at night took on even more poise and power. That power could not be extinguished, she thought, for it was rooted in a society charged with energy. It dawned on her that the wave of resurgence, sweeping a world of great change, would be stronger than the wave of destruction of the pandemic, despite the cold winds that still blew. She could see that in New York a powerful determination to go forward was flowing in the minds of those at the forefront of the innovative sectors.

The next morning, she visited some art galleries that had reopened near the Guggenheim. She was shocked by the high prices of all the works. One of the gallery owners explained to her that the rich were buying at an accelerated pace. They were afraid that the stock market would crash and real estate taxes would rise, so they were looking at investing in art as a valuable alternative. As she left, she thought that the market was insatiable, and reflected on the many different layers that existed in society. She remembered Paul Éluard›s phrase, 'There is another world, but it is in this one.' Then she left for the airport to catch her flight to Mexico. She went through all the checkpoints, which had now become very strict because the American authorities had finally decided to thoroughly identify anyone who could be infected. After a long wait, she boarded the Aeromexico flight. She liked that company because it offered very personable treatment.

She settled in comfortably and ordered Mexican food off the menu as soon as the plane took off. She loved chili peppers and everything that was a little spicy. Remembering moments from her recent experience in New York, she slept peacefully for the rest of the trip and her dreams brought her back to the centre of discussions about the future of the world.

Chapter 18

The Astronaut's Testimony

THE MAN who had seen the world from the outside took the floor. What a privilege to have been able to see the beauty of the Earth from the heavenly body that illuminates us at night! The man had come to walk on the surface of the moon when his eyes shone with all their intensity, when his heart scarcely stirred, when his brain could process spatial manipulation. He now came to the rostrum with a tired appearance, the indelible mark of old age, but with his courage intact, to present a unique testament to the value of humanity. He began his brief message with a short but emphatic sentence, 'Yes, dear friends, we did it!'

And a thunderous applause from the whole audience interrupted him. In just a few words he had made it clear how great and wonderful humanity was, and the feats it can achieve when it rises to its most powerful dimension, intelligence.

When the emotion of all those present calmed down, he continued with his speech. 'The dream handed down from generation to generation since the birth of humankind—to get to know the heavenly body that illuminates us at night and seems deceptively within our reach when it emerges from the horizon—my colleagues and I were able to unveil it. What is up there is the ability to see the most beautiful planet in the universe.' Again, the audience thundered with applause. When he could be heard again, he continued:

'My first thought as I set foot on the dead, grey dust, was to think of the beauty of our native land. I said to myself, how could I imagine the diversity of our own planet if I had been born on this drab satellite? What a privilege we have, to inhabit such a beautiful place! I took several steps to test my ability to walk on a surface without gravity, and then I managed to travel a few hundred meters with the small vehicle that NASA had designed. I took samples of various moon rocks that all had the same appearance, the same configuration, one after the other. What struck me the most was that the immensity of that desert space had no soul. And someone may well ask: "How could it have a soul if it was desert?" And I want to tell that person that I have not found a place on Earth with a deeper soul than the deserts. We live on an extraordinary planet.'

His words were accompanied by a moment of silence despite the enthusiastic applause earlier. He continued: 'I have never enjoyed greater harmony than the days I spent alone in the red desert, south of Ouarzazate, preparing to walk on the lunar desert. On our Earth, there is the most precious gift in the universe, life, and this must be the good that is placed at the centre of our existence. Preserve it, enhance it for all of us! Life is the only thing that should matter to us in our brief passage on this marvellous planet Earth. We must see the numerous existing differences and problems as different faces of a diamond.

'Or, is not the most coveted diamond the one that has the largest number of cubes in it, and thus breaks up the light in the most perfect way? We must see our existence in the same way. We are vectors of life, and difference is our greatest source of wealth.

'I remember how awestruck we, the three astronauts, were when we returned. We hardly uttered a word during the three days we spent on our way back from space. We had discovered the grandeur of humanity! This is what I am here to testify to today, and I ask you once again for ambition and wisdom; we are unique in our ability to fly higher than our dreams.' And once again the whole hall vibrated with thunderous applause. For many minutes everyone was carried away by the emotion of recognising human greatness in a palpable way.

When everyone calmed down, he continued:

'The nearer I came to Earth, the more I felt a great uneasiness, for I was tormented by the thought of not being able to communicate to the world what I had learned in the seconds of eternity I had enjoyed. But that time has come today! Although this has happened half a century ago and I have explained it on countless occasions, it is today that I feel that I am communicating it with all its intensity to those who can convert it into the energy of progress. This is because I am explaining it in the fertile ground of a humanity that wants to forge a path in a new world, fixed on growing in harmony and developing the era of intelligence. A world that seeks the path of holistic grandeur. A great moment without a doubt, and my happiness is at its highest, for the god Kronos has allowed me to endure decade after decade with this mission. Yes, we are a wonderful species, and we must think of our central root, to be one humanity. Differences are only nuances that give colour to the big picture. And so, I join in the plea of the speakers before me, that this magnificent audience finds the formula that will bring us together in a new political architecture that transcends the narrow confines of nations, defuses the artificial tensions created by dividing ourselves into groups, and liberates our life under a new system of governance that aims at a creative peace, where each individual is called to create and discover. Since I returned from space, we have certainly come a long way. We have brought down the Iron Curtain and overcome the Cold War, this noble organisation has adopted such landmark documents as the Millennium Development Goals and the 2030 Agenda, and the world has been endowed with great technological advances. However, we are still sitting on a powder keg, and we continue to maintain the political centre of gravity in groups and states. That is why my call contains an urgent appeal—let us be smart and build a world in which everyone contributes to making a jewel of our planet unequalled.'

His words did not have the flavour of the naivety of one who is beginning life, but of the wisdom of a man in his twilight, who has seen the miracle of humanity from the cosmos. Yet again, applause filled the hall, and descending from the rostrum with a humble air, he gave way to the next speaker.

Chapter 19

To Mexico

Extrasensory perception: Navigating through the past and the future

NOUR LANDED in Mexico City in the early afternoon. As she flew over the city, it occurred to her that because of its broad expansion this city was the closest thing to a human sea. It stretched out flat for miles and miles. It was the largest inhabited immensity she had ever known. She thought of how large it had been in ancient times. When the Spanish explorers arrived after landing at Veracruz, Mexico was a city of four hundred thousand inhabitants at a time when London, Paris, and Rome each had less than one hundred thousand. The Federal District was a metropolitan area articulated around seven hills, and the space in between was a navigable lake. The Aztecs moved with canoes from one hill to another. The scholars and historians of the past claimed that it was the most beautiful Venice ever built by mankind. Now the lake's water had been diverted and the formerly muddy areas were new neighbourhoods crammed with houses that were fragile in the face of earthquakes, but which provided shelter to an endless human magma.

During the last congress she had attended in the Mexican capital, she had met a young artificial intelligence researcher named Emiliano Rodriguez, who had told her about the power of the shamans and their visionary abilities.

He also mentioned to her the mastery of the ancient cultures of America, the Aztecs, Mayas, and Incas, of the power of certain herbs with which to contact other dimensions of life. She had been passionate about the subject, but lack of time had prevented her from experiencing it. Now, she had found the opportunity to explore this experience. She had contacted Emiliano and told him about the possibility of coming from New York. Mexico had been badly affected by the pandemic, but it had not been closed to air traffic with the United States, and she was able to arrange the trip. The response she received cleared up any doubts. With his usual enthusiasm, Emiliano told her that all she had to do was to get there. He would have everything ready.

Nour thanked him, began to plan the trip, and thought of the warmth she always perceived in the Mexican people. How could they always have that capacity for enthusiasm, that empathy, even in difficult moments? She remembered that in the course of her difficult experience of emigration, after leaving Damascus, she was often told of the unequalled welcome that the Mexicans had extended to Spanish exiles during the civil war. In those difficult times, President Cárdenas ordered all the customs workers to not only welcome any Spaniard who arrived with open arms, but also to find out their line of work and to stamp their passport with permission to carry out that profession. This greatly facilitated the integration of the exiles. No other country had the courage to make such a commitment and authoritatively solve a problem that would otherwise continue to worsen.

These same émigrés were interned in refugee camps in France, or were only tolerated, but without being given any facilities for integration in many other countries of America. Nour had benefited from the solidarity in much of German society, but the authorities had been unable to make her experience of integration as rapid and positive as President Cárdenas had in the days when the Spaniards crossed the Atlantic barrier. That story, which was always recurring in emigrant circles, now came to mind while she landed in Mexico.

She passed through the controls without difficulty and found Emiliano waiting for her, standing at the arrivals barrier with a huge bouquet of flowers. He said to her jokingly:

'I could have found a bigger one but not a more beautiful one, and I hope you like it, for you deserve no less after crossing not only half of America but half of the world, from what you told me!'

She had not expected this, but, always sensitive to the generosity of feelings, she thanked him with all her heart:

'They're beautiful. I couldn't have made a better entrance into Mexico,' she said before giving him an affectionate kiss on the cheek.

'You know, Emiliano? When we said goodbye at the end of the last congress, I always thought that our meeting would be the first of many. I'm glad that now the occasion has arrived.' They soon reached the car. Compared to the hustle and bustle of crowds and activity that the airport used to be, it was now empty and Emiliano had been able to park very close.

They walked along the Paseo de la Reforma and, after turning at the historic centre, they arrived at Emiliano's apartment, located in the Condesa district. This was where young people with possibilities went to live, but they were not, as the Mexicans said, 'strawberries' or children of rich families, but young people with momentum, from struggling and upwardly mobile middle-class families. His apartment was pleasant, and overlooked a small park where the jacaranda trees sported beautiful blue-violet flowers. 'This is your home for as long as you want,' he said as he showed her what would be her room.

She had flown more than six hours, passing through very strict controls. Due to the pandemic, the air traffic in the United States had become very rigid, multiplying the procedures to identify possibly infected people. Everything had been cumbersome at the New York airport, and what she wanted most of all was a good shower.

'If you don't mind,' she said, 'I'll take a nice shower.'

'Of course,' he replied, 'that will do you good.'

She threw everything that she had on across the floor of her bathroom and gladly reached under the big showerhead to turn the taps on full blast. The water gushed out powerfully and she felt the satisfaction one feels when things work well. She lathered herself thoroughly and, as the water hit every part of her body, an irrepressible desire came over her. It was a young soul's desire, why not allow herself a little madness in a world that had become so distant? 'He's very fine,' she said to herself. 'He's tall, with strong arms and full lips that incite pleasure.' Sensual images and delicious caresses crossed her imagination. She finished the shower, pulled on a pair of light shorts and went to sit next to Emiliano, who had prepared a tequila and lime for her in the living room. He began to explain in detail the itinerary he had prepared. They would leave very early the next morning because the shaman wanted to meet her at sunrise and the village was quite a few kilometres from the Federal District.

They talked about the advances in the new artificial intelligence systems that were being developed in Mexico, and she experienced waves of desire as he talked, watching his hands and his long, strong, nervous fingers that spoke of intensity and pleasure. As the afternoon wore on, she could not stop thinking about all the time she had spent without making love. In Germany the anti-contagion measures had been draconian and no one had been able to leave their rooms for months. Only in the heart of Siberia, at the end of her stay in Novosibirsk, and during the crossing of the desert to Dakar, had she been able to enjoy the pleasure of love again. With Emiliano, desire was beginning to overflow; it was beyond calculation. She felt sexually alive again, seized by a rapturous desire beyond all foresight.

The tequila had been accompanying the whole conversation and the current of electricity had been growing between them as their confidence grew. Finally, she decided to open the game without further ado. 'You know, Emiliano, with this pandemic we've all become so stagnant, so stuck in our nature, that we've already begun to live like beings with a mind but without instincts, almost like beings of artificial intelligence,' and they both laughed, unable to stop. 'And now I am experiencing the opposite. I'm seized by a mad desire to make love to you. An irrepressible desire to kiss you and to enjoy without limits or fears.'

In that small apartment in the Condesa, two deep forces of human nature intersected, the sensual passion of the Arab world and the attractive and somewhat salacious intensity of the Mexican soul. Emiliano did not answer her with words but with actions. He stood up, elegantly removed the light t-shirt she had put on, which in the heat had become soaked, revealing her beautiful breasts, and kissed her while she let her long hair fall back. They were long, sensual kisses that excited her even more, and he took her in his arms to lay her on the bed.

She looked at him then with a confident gaze and tenderly said, 'Enter like an emperor into the gardens of a queen.' And then she added, 'You know, in these times when the distance between all of us is so predominant, when we are horrified at the thought of the risks we can take, to be able to enjoy the passion of sex again, this wonderful dimension of life that we must not renounce, is a gift worthy of the gods. I was born into a world that lived intensely in love and passion and luckily this seed lives on in my soul. Enjoying the pleasure that floods us, like a storm that soaks us through, is just marvellous. And all my blood, numbed by an education based on control, is waking up today like a volcano. Come closer and love me as much as you want tonight, initiating the liturgy of love in a delicious way, so that I absorb each of your raptures and my body enjoys each convulsion.'

They made love all night long. Her body was blessed with the best age. She still had the strength of youth, but the years had given her enough experience to bring out the complicity of man, inciting him to give himself to the art of love. It was an unforgettable night for them, and it brought them closer than ever to the depths of their souls. It gave way to a deep friendship, noble and full of mutual understanding, opening the door to be able to communicate directly and sincerely in the future.

Early, before dawn, they left for Malinalco, past Cuernavaca, where the shaman was waiting for them. As they climbed the hill to Cuernavaca, on a completely empty road, feeling like they were the only living beings in motion, they could see the flickering immensity of Mexico City. If by day it looked like an immense sea, at night it grew even larger until it seemed to be a scale model of the universe, with all the tiny twinkling dots as the thousands of stars populating it. 'It's a wonder that everything can function in this immensity and that all the houses have light, that everything turns on and off every day,' thought Nour, while Emiliano drove in silence, wondering how the meeting with the shaman would unfold. They finally arrived at the shaman's hut in Malinalco, located next to the ceremonial centre of Cuauhcalli, on the hill of the Idols, on the top of the volcanic rock. They parked at the foot of the hill and climbed the four hundred and twenty steps that convert the ascent to the summit into an almost mystical preparation for the imminent meeting. The shaman was an older, burly man, with a very large head, thick fingers, and a strong but not obese build. He greeted them with a slight movement of his face to indicate that he was waiting for them and that he was ready.

Emiliano explained that Nour did not speak Spanish, but they would understand each other through the little device she carried which translated instantly and accurately. The shaman suggested that she could even speak in her native language of Otomi and she agreed, immediately adjusting the program of her device to this German-Otomi language combination. Emiliano left, and Nour and the shaman were alone. He looked at her for a few minutes and finally asked her:

'Do you really want me to tell you the future?' And she responded with a half-answer:

'That impresses me. I don't want to know it in detail, I couldn't live with a life whose chapters were already written, but I would like to know your power and experience how you connect with the future.'

Looking at her very steadily for a long time, he told her that he did not know the extent of his abilities and how his power of connection with the future worked, but it was certainly a dimension he had, just as one who can see, smell, and hear. Instead of limiting himself to the more immediate senses, he could see through time and interpret the signs that came to him.

The sun was rising over the temple and the light was advancing rapidly. She asked him if she had to give him any information and he said no, that it was enough for her to maintain eye contact and let herself be completely penetrated by his gaze. He then prepared the herbs in a small bowl and took small sips of the ayahuasca. In the Aztec tradition, they believe that plants speak; ayahuasca has the virtue of whispering the deep truths of others. Then he stood for a few long minutes staring openly at her and let his predictions unravel.

'I see,' he said to her, 'that you have come down a long sea, which resembles a very wide river, stretching out like a tongue, opening out into a greater sea, where there is an island. The mist that envelops it causes the greatest shipwrecks to those who are not extremely vigilant. I see also, that coming from far away, you left your father behind. Shortly you will arrive at a large, immense island, and, before leaving, you will receive the sad news of his death. He will die in his sleep. You will not suffer because you love him, and you will know that fate will have taken him in the best way.'

Nour's face saddened as she kept thinking about the shaman's abilities. How could he have described so well a recent episode in her life, and how could he dare to make such a detailed and concrete prediction of the future? As far as the past was concerned, he had been right, and as far as the future was concerned, she hoped he was not, but if he was, it raised a big question mark about the limits of cognitive ability. It opened up a new field about the explorable limits of artificial intelligence. 'If we humans have this ability to tune into time and space in the past and the future,' she reckoned, 'artificial intelligence may be able to go beyond that in the future, and thereby further transform the history and evolution of humankind.'

She and the shaman exchanged gestures of farewell, and Nour went back down the four hundred and twenty steps to find Emiliano and return to Mexico City. She went down with a troubled soul, hoping that the prediction about her father would not come true, especially when she had left him enjoying the quietest and most peaceful period of his life as the pandemic had confined him for a few months without any workload.

Moreover, the virus had fortunately not affected him, and now the doctors knew a little more about how to control it. Gradually, she became calmer and at the same time fascinated by how the mind could penetrate the past and the future. She reached the end of the long descent and climbed into the car where Emiliano had been waiting for her for more than an hour. They drove back and soon she began to talk about the man's magic. She told Emiliano nothing of his predictions, nor did he, out of delicacy, ask her.

'You know,' she began, 'the impressive thing about this is that I have come to understand the power of tuning. I wonder how far we could go in this field with the new artificial intelligence entities we will create in the future. It seems to me an immense field to explore and one of boundless potential. The experience with the shaman is equivalent to being in a silent space and suddenly being able to rely on a transistor. We see nothing and hear nothing without it, but the space is full of music, of discourses, of thousands of different registers. And without the transistor what do we have—silence. All that which floats in space is there without us even suspecting it. But it only requires a tuner to immediately start living in another universe. Instantly we pick up symphonies, historical speeches, news, and so on, an endless number of voices that transport us to other moments. The shaman has this ability to tune in, just as the dowser can identify the exact point of a subterranean stream of water and its flow even if it is a hundred metres deep and there is no external sign that indicates it.

'I am impressed by the powers of our mind, which are largely untapped, but which undoubtedly exist. The shaman has gone into the past and it is as if everything I have experienced is imprisoned in my soul, just as when we start to work on a computer everything is recorded on its hard disk, even if we later erase it from the screen and no longer see it with the naked eye. But someone with far superior technical knowledge can retrieve it, because nothing that enters disappears. It is definitively inserted into the life of the machine. And our brain and our soul act perhaps in the same way as the computer.

'We go through life thinking that the past has been the way to get to the present and we keep it in the form of memories. But that past may not remain as a dead product, rather it may climb into our soul and become part of the living dimensions of our person. It involves energies that others pick up, perhaps without decoding them exactly, but they perceive them. The impressive thing about the shaman is that he is able to decode them and bring the past back to the present in all its forms. I have been fascinated by this power of attainment. Regarding the future, it is even more impressive for it is not we who carry it, but time. The events are already floating in time, like a distant branch of the river floating down. They are a point that we will inevitably reach later, and although we neither see it nor imagine it, the shaman, like a bird that crosses space at greater speed, glimpses it before it envelops us. He can thus penetrate time! And I think that our artificial intelligence entities will be able to do it even more impressively.'

'Of course, it's a virgin field for us,' Emiliano told her. 'We'll have to research how the brain can enter the future and the past, and from there develop the algorithms that replicate it exponentially.'

Then she took an even more ambitious tack.

Somewhat shaken but excited, she told him:

'Can you imagine the new world we would enter if the decisions we make were not only based on more or less immediate forecasts, but also on their consequences thousands of years in the future for generations of new millennia? We would be living in immense complexity.

It would be a total change of dimension. And if when the telephone, electricity, or airplanes were invented, those who lived through it thought that the world had undergone a radical change, now the change would be even greater. We would move into the future dimension from the present dimension based on the information provided by artificial intelligence. It is a challenge for our generation, the first that will put the exponential advances of artificial intelligence into practice.'

Nour stayed in Mexico for the whole week. They were unforgettable days as she enjoyed every single moment shared with Emiliano. During the day they discussed new topics in the development of artificial intelligence systems. Afternoons were spent in the Condesa, the vibrant district of Mexico City, where Emiliano introduced her to friends who soon grew close to Nour. That was one of the advantages of Mexico—the enormous empathy of its people.

She discovered there the value of friendship as she had not experienced before.

But finally, she had to leave, and it was difficult for her to say goodbye. She promised Emiliano that she would return regularly to Mexico, and they would start a thousand future projects, because she felt very much at home there, especially now after having started such a strong friendship. She didn't want to leave, but the car that was supposed to take her to the airport began to beep insistently from the street, and she had to go. She couldn't delay any longer because the flight to Tokyo was leaving in a couple of hours and, although there were no queues at the airport and crossing the city didn't cost anything, the health and safety formalities were cumbersome and time-consuming.

'I'm sorry to have kept you waiting, but parting is always difficult in a sincere friendship,' she said by way of explanation to the driver as she got into the car.

'It'll be tight, but we'll be just in time,' he answered her succinctly.

All went well and soon she found herself seated on the Japan Air Jumbo bound for Tokyo. It was a long trip, but it would pass quickly as it was night-time. On take-off, she could see the vastness of Mexico City from the air once again. Then she chose one of her favourite movies, *A Night on Earth*, and after an excellent sashimi dinner accompanied by hot sake, she fell asleep. Soon dreams took her back to the great hall of the Palais des Nations, where discussions were intense and delegates prepared what would be their countries' response speeches.

Chapter 20

The Hour Of The New Ruler

THE MAN who was developing artificial intelligence systems to manage public affairs took the floor. He was a young man, hurried in his communication, whose brain seemed to be moving much faster than his mouth could articulate his ideas. He stepped up to the podium, adjusting his blue-rimmed glasses and settled with aplomb in front of the microphone. 'It is an honour for me to be here today before this great audience,' he said.

'I have always dreamed of this moment, but I never thought it would come so quickly. Just as wars open the door to great changes, this pandemic may be opening the door to better thinking about how to organise our societies and, above all, how to organise our collective life on the planet. I believe that the contribution of artificial intelligence could be fundamental, and I would like to explain why. Until now power has been concentrated in the hands of leaders, and they have tended to organise societies on the basis of ideas, beliefs, and customs. Little data has been used to maximise everyone's potential and also to achieve the best interrelationship among all of us. This has led to the blind management of societies, in contrast to the perfection with which they could be managed.

'Artificial intelligence systems are now opening the door to better management of societies. We have started to use them in cities to regulate mobility much more intelligently. States must now quickly move in this direction. Their management teams must change radically. The administrations have played an important role in ensuring objectivity, honesty, and transparency in the management of public programs. However, they lack the agility and initiative that these modern times require. Obviously, we need final decision-makers to set the course, but all the enormous work of preparing decisions, analysing needs, and offering solutions to each emerging problem must come from artificial intelligence teams. Big data must not only be introduced but be generalised in public administration, so that citizens find an optimal playing field for the development of their initiatives. Then, having achieved this, we must go further.

'We must create algorithms that help mobilise energy and initiatives across the planet. The dynamics of groups must be left behind. The future lies in making each individual a great entrepreneur, a being who contributes through new initiatives and develops projects. And for this we must organise the world with a system of global government. And today we have the basis, the organisation that you lead, Secretary-General, which is undoubtedly a great historical milestone. It is the most advanced public body that humanity has been able to put in place to govern itself as a whole.

'But since its creation after the Second World War, the world has changed a great deal. It was born in 1945 with fifty-two nations and today has more than 190 members. It was born in a world divided by ideology and today it is a world without ideological fracture but with multiple uncertainties. We are, therefore, at a transcendental crossroads. We are either setting out on the road towards Great History or we are disintegrating like a sugar cube in the misery of grudges and petty struggles, lurching like a disoriented bird and destroying much of what we have achieved. To move forward today means that from this great organisation we should move to a world administration where the control panel is in human hands, but is controlled by artificial intelligence systems at all operational levels. It will be a revolution of human intelligence for knowing how to organise itself as a whole. Moreover, it will be a revolution at the hands of artificial intelligence and its ability to combine data on the most diverse realities, needs, and opportunities on a global scale, and to propose ways of constantly regulating these changing realities that lead to maximising the results of everything and for everyone.'

Absolute silence and great expectation gripped everyone in the room. This man was clearly explaining to them how the future was going to be, and his degree of concreteness announced that he would go even further in his speech. He drank some water to prepare for the final part of his speech. In a clear voice and a slower tone, he continued:

'I will present to this attentive audience the five concrete cases of how much we must change.

'The first case: During the pandemic, no country has ever managed to mobilise all its vast resources. Never have medical universities been more crowded and rarely has there been a generation so eager to help. However, no student has been called upon to take samples, to track cases, or to care for the sick personally. Never has the number of epidemiologists been greater, but they have all continued to be separated by their nationalities. The enormous data that has been available has gone unprocessed in most cases. In short, public affairs continue to be dominated by ego, interpersonal feuds, and jealousy, and recruitment systems by slow and cumbersome procedures. As a result, we have fallen behind the times, and a simple virus has put the whole world in jeopardy. What are we waiting for to learn and correct course by introducing artificial intelligence into civil service?

'Second case: The future of mobility in the world is

in the open skies. When we all fly single-seaters through the air and all transport is airborne, we will not need to maintain any fixed infrastructure. Trains and cars, along with the heavy circuits of streets, roads, highways, motorways, and tracks will all be obsolete. We should not see this as a distant future, but we need to have open space in the whole world. Are we preparing for this? The technical systems will soon be ready, but are we going to be ready in terms of regulation and management? Any delay will have a huge impact on our ability to develop and a huge cost in maintenance and pollution. With artificial intelligence systems we could be prepared for that future, so what are we waiting for?

'Third case: The world has progressed a lot, leaving behind illiteracy, and exponentially multiplying compulsory education systems. But we are still attached to tradition, to teaching too many things that do not sink in and to forgetting others that are crucial to learn. Using artificial intelligence systems and big data, we must review what we are doing, its results, and the desire for what we would like to have. Their diagnosis will be shattering. We will discover how much energy we are wasting on students and trainees and how many opportunities to develop talent we are missing. What are we waiting for to move in the right direction?

'Fourth case: One of the great problems in achieving a better geographical distribution of populations and in advancing along the path of good urban planning is in land ownership systems. But most legal reforms lead to conflicts or result in measures that create new inequalities or stagnate activity. We usually work with a great lack of data. We need to rethink this whole issue and develop new models based on the cross-referencing of data and the results we would like to achieve. We need to innovate in this area and leave behind rigid visions driven by overly conceptual ideologies. What are we waiting for to innovate?

'Fifth case: A great step forward for everyone would be the ability to administer justice quickly and accurately. However, in the vast majority of countries, the opposite is true. Justice is slow and procedurally heavy. We must use the energy and wisdom of judges to focus on the essentials of judgements and to use systems of artificial intelligence to process most of the issues they have to resolve. A justice system that gains in objectivity and speed will enhance security and human dignity, and artificial intelligence can contribute a great deal to this. What are we waiting for to make immediate progress in this field?

'I do not wish, eminent delegates, to waste either your time or your patience. We could spend days and days analysing the potential of artificial intelligence in many fields. I wanted briefly to underline that today there is a world coming to an end in the conduct of public affairs and a new one emerging. We could say that the world has, up until now, undergone a convulsive but quite controlled evolution. Now all capacities are accelerating, and the management of collective aspirations requires a great understanding of everyone's expectations and possibilities that only artificial intelligence systems can integrate, arbitrate, and channel. We can no longer delay the introduction of the necessary changes. We have a promising road ahead of us. I trust that we will all walk this path and open up great horizons for the new generations.'

Applause filled the hall, and the speaker, grateful for the standing ovation, stepped down from the rostrum with a humble air and gave way to the representatives of the states who were to speak on the new direction to be taken. The time had come for those who had to take the step forward, thus opening the door to the future.

Chapter 21

Towards The Empire Of The Rising Sun

The world as a derived reality

NOUR ARRIVED in Tokyo at dawn. The city always reminded her of the film *Blade Runner*, with its mixture of modernity and stealth. It was curious how a culture that had been so delicate and traditional in the past had created a city after the Second World War that served as the ultimate example for the future. It was a city where the visual impact of the large advertisements on top of the buildings, imposing their presence, is combined with a touch of inscrutable secrecy. This duality creates a halo of mystery and a certain irreality. It is very different from the feeling one gets in New York, also the capital of modernity, where the great wheel of mass consumption is made evident. There, everything feels vertiginous, temporary, and somewhat one-dimensional. Tokyo is the other side of modernity. It is so impenetrable that it is the capital of mysterious lights and shadows. Nour had been there many times before to participate in world congresses on artificial intelligence and she loved the city. She connected there to the future and subtlety.

But she had never known it so empty, so deserted as it was this time. 'This disaster has permeated everything like a great tsunami,' she thought. She was glad, however, that in these times of great upheaval in the world, she could meet again with Asahi, the great Japanese master in the field of artificial intelligence, who was ready to teach her about the great new project he had told her about the previous year.

Because of his age, now approaching ninety, he was confined to his home, but he was delighted to answer in the affirmative her question about spending a few days together: 'My great pupil, my light in the universe,' he said, referencing the meaning of her name, 'of course, you can come and, moreover, stay at my home, for your energy will bring a little life back into these dark times. Now I have plenty of time, and we can talk at length about all the questions which are opening up for our science.'

Asahi had introduced her to the most promising fields of artificial intelligence during the master class he had given in Hamburg six years ago, and since then his advice had always guided her through the crucial moments of her research. However, his obligations as a consultant to many Asian governments prevented him from spending more than a few minutes with her at conferences. Now she had the opportunity to spend not only hours but a few days with him. As the taxi pulled into the Asakusa district, Nour experienced a mixture of joy and serenity, a harbinger of what was to be a great meeting.

She lifted the copper knocker hanging in the centre of the door, and Aiko, Asahi's maid, soon opened it and welcomed her with a delicate smile. She had been taking care of Asahi for the past thirty years and, thanks to her, he could live alone in his world of the future. The present rested perfectly in Aiko's hands.

The house retained all the character of traditional Tokyo. Fortunately, it had not been destroyed during the war, and it was a little gem among the new, tall buildings in the neighbourhood. At the back was a large garden with countless bonsai trees and as well as a large covered pavilion. She went upstairs with Aiko to the top floor where Asahi retired to read during the day. He rose as she entered, and they greeted each other in the Japanese style, not touching but reflecting the satisfaction of seeing each other. Immediately the teacher asked Aiko to bring up some green tea and some dorayakis, stuffed pancakes, to welcome Nour.

'I'm so glad you're here. I imagine you must be tired after such a long journey,' he said.

'I slept well on the plane, but a little rest will do me good, although I can't wait to learn about what you're doing.'

'We'll have time, Nour, don't worry,' he said. 'Everything is at a standstill, and it's good to take advantage of this downtime to address things without rushing. I've asked Aiko to prepare the room on the middle floor for you, where I think you'll do very well. Now, we can have green tea. When you've finished, rest until the early evening, and then we'll go for a little walk, if you like.'

Aiko came in with a beautiful antique ceramic tea set and some dorayakis that tasted glorious. They drank the tea quietly, and then Nour went to rest until early evening.

At five o'clock, Nour and Asahi went for a walk around Asakusa, a neighbourhood that still retained much of its traditional Japanese character despite the large modern buildings beginning to impact the area.

Asahi walked slowly but upright despite his advanced age. He always liked to take this walk before dinner, for it was like a relaxing pause. In the morning, he would read, and in the evening, between supper and bedtime, he would do research. 'I always walk through these streets,' Asahi would say to her as they walked along without going anywhere in particular. 'They make me think about how we should face the future. You'll see that some old houses like mine still survive, reflecting a detailed and legendary culture. Then there are these tall buildings that reflect a Japan that is far from its course but which has also been able to innovate. Now must come the third phase, in which we aim to be among the leaders in artificial intelligence and develop a new model of coexistence, combining the benefits of futurism with a calmer pace of life, in line with our tradition of being precise and meticulous.' As they passed by the shops selling flowers and bonsai, he leisurely explained to her the intimate connection of the Japanese with nature.

They returned home for dinner. Aiko had prepared a seaweed soup and vegetable tempura, Asahi's favourite dishes. They sat down quietly, and Asahi began to explain his latest research in progress:

"Tomorrow, I will show you something that will surprise you. It ties in with my reflection on the limits of life and the difference or similarity between us and the beings we will create with artificial intelligence.'

'It will be hard for me to wait until tomorrow,' she said. 'With that on the horizon, I don't know if I'll be able to sleep. I have often wondered what the limits of what we will create might be, and it seems that tomorrow I will have an enlightening clue for the first time.'

'Well, don't expect so much, though perhaps you'll get some first insights,' Asahi told her with a placid, wise smile on his lips.

The next day passed quietly. Nour used the morning to visit the city's two main contemporary art museums and the photography museum. Japan was at the forefront of contemporary art, and the two museums' exhibits were spectacular. Nour enjoyed it immensely because, due to the pandemic, visitor capacity was reduced, so one could enjoy the uncrowded viewing of the paintings in each room. Her visit to the photography museum was also wonderful. She was an unconditional admirer of Hiroshi Sugimoto and Masao Yamamoto, and the museum housed a large body of their work. She admired Sugimoto's photographs of the sea and the horizon to no end. They were powerful and intriguing, capturing time, caught in the intersection of ocean and horizon. She was also fascinated by how Yamamoto could capture the flight of birds so well, even capturing the personalities of each bird in flight! 'What two great photographers!' she thought every time she looked at their work. 'Japanese culture is so respectful of detail and perfection that their photographers are giants of art. They are defined by incomparable excellence,' she said to herself as she descended the stairs of the museum to get into a taxi and return home.

In the afternoon, after tea in the library, Asahi invited her to see the project he had mentioned.

They went downstairs and he took her to the big shed he had built in the garden. Her jaw dropped as he opened the door. There, Asahi had created a new miniature planet, where the new generation of beings interacted with each other. He had recreated autonomous entities that lived like the beings we know, but artificial, interacting with each other like humans and even reproducing. 'I have the key to their existence, but I'm not convinced that one day they won't become so intelligent that they reach a high degree of autonomy, and create their own world with new beings derived from them. That world will no longer be directly related to me and will orbit in a new artificial universe like this one, in which they will feel they are the protagonists. Thus is created an endless chain of beings and derived worlds,' he said in deep voice.

She was stunned. She had always wondered about the limits of artificial intelligence and whether one day the new beings could overpower humans, but what Asahi was showing her was superior. It was the creation of a complete universe that was believed to be real but was actually a programmed creation. More importantly, if the new beings became so intelligent that they created new beings and new universes, couldn't the whole vast complexity of the universe follow the same pattern? Couldn't we be virtual beings created by other virtual beings in a universe that seemed real to us when in reality it had all been programmed by other beings? The experience fascinated her and made her dizzy at the same time. It fascinated her because it opened up an immense field. It made her dizzy because it made her doubt her very existence and who she really was!

She had entered the field of artificial intelligence fascinated by what it meant for the future, and artificial intelligence, reaching its most advanced point as Asahi was now showing her, was now sending her back to the past, to the great metaphysics that the Greeks had embodied, wondering about the essence of life.

'It is fascinating how these beings live what they consider to be their own lives,' he said, pointing to an artificial being, who appeared to be very young, complaining to an older one about demanding too much of him. 'You have to observe,' he reasoned with a certain irony this time, 'how beings who are nothing but simply the product of my mind, when given advanced emotional dimensions, begin to act with expectations and become happy or sad depending on how the other artificial beings interact with them. They believe in their life when they are nothing more than a virtual projection created by me.'

They lingered for a long time watching the artificial mini-universe. In the evening they went to a nearby restaurant with a reputation for good sake and good sashimi for dinner.

'You know, I'm very old now,' Asahi said, 'but today I want to indulge in a little sake with you. I want to make a hopeful wish—that what you've seen today can be perfected in the years to come, and that your generation will be ground-breaking in this respect! I'm at the end, but you're just beginning a very promising trip.'

She shed some tears of emotion over the confidence that the one she considered the great master was showing her, and also of admiration for what he had achieved.

'You know, Asahi, my generation will not fail you,'

she replied, tenderly taking his hand. 'In spite of the deep setback of the pandemic we will not lose momentum, I promise you! It is true that there is a long way to go, but we will devote ourselves to it. This terrible pandemic has destroyed many things and, above all, fond habits, such as the physical closeness between people, but it forces us to move forward with new dimensions. I have no doubt that this will be a prolific field. I am fascinated by the idea of thinking not only of beings, but of macro-systems that reproduce a whole universe starring artificially intelligent creatures. How far we will be able to control the chain is the big open question, but I think it will be fascinating to explore it in depth and to venture into it without knowing the end.'

He looked at her with eyes of gratitude, relief, and happiness at knowing that she had picked up his baton. Outside it was raining lightly; like someone who savours closing a chapter that has been long and complex, they slowly crossed a few streets hand in hand and returned inside the house.

That night Nour slept peacefully. Asahi had shown her the extent to which the beings of the universe could be the concatenation of many civilisations derived from other, all artificial. Civilisations which, believing themselves to be living their own determining experiences, were nothing more than the experimentation of a previous and superior one. It all seemed so tremendous and complex that she chose to embrace stoicism and fall asleep in the utmost tranquillity. And, in that state, she re-entered the great hall where the future architecture of the world was being debated and where now it was the turn of the delegates of the countries to respond to the challenge of advancing towards a single humanity.

Chapter 22

From The World Split Into Nations To The World United In One Humanity

ONE BY one the delegates of the countries representing the whole world in the great assembly took the floor. The speaker who embodied one of the most ancient cultures, the Arab world, now deeply torn apart, was the first to go to the rostrum.

'I speak, Secretary-General,' began a tall, strong man with a deep voice, a thick beard, and a forehead furrowed with heavy wrinkles, 'on behalf of a vast number of countries in a great region of the world, united at times by language and ambition, at others by history and values, and which today are at a difficult crossroads, beset by deep differences and divisions. In the current moment of history, we find ourselves facing many unresolved conflicts, and we are in a state of despondency, because we do not know how to find the way forward that will set us on a grander footing for the future. We occupy the region where the various civilisations that have inhabited it have brought wisdom and progress to the world. What kingdom was more sublime than the Iraq of the gardens of Babylon, the Egypt of Pharaohs, or the Persia of Darius with the marvel of Persepolis? But now we circle and circle again around our weaknesses without finding the strength to bring out the brilliance of our creativity and restore our splendour. After the arrival of Muhammad, Islam took hold in the region and brought much to humanity.

'Great scholars such as Averroes innovated in medicine; others, such as Al Khwarizmi and Al-Battani, in algebra and astronomy. A long number of contributions in all fields of science, literature, and the arts, have left an outstanding architectural legacy of sublime beauty.

'While the West lived through times of pain and darkness, the drive and vision of our sages maintained the progress of humanity. Today, however, we are in a period of great tensions and ruptures. In the last two centuries, the domination of the West, *de facto* or *de jure*, over many of our countries has created a major impasse in our history. And it is into the heart of this upheaval that many of our modern borders were arbitrarily drawn, displacing populations and artificially creating States. A dramatic result is the suffering of the Palestinian people who were removed from their land during the creation of Israel, without a prior international conference to seal an agreement and make such action acceptable.

'There are many difficulties in the life of our nations

today. We are experiencing major internal religious failures, as the West experienced for centuries, and which resulted in continual internal wars. We experience the separation of religious and civil matters at different rates in different countries. Tze economy differs like night and day between those who are born with abundant natural resources and those who have not been equally favoured. But it is true that, as the great civilisation that we were, there is nothing to prevent our citizens from once again being among the most creative on Earth. Perhaps, what we are failing to achieve as nations, we can achieve as spaces inserted in global governance.

'It will be difficult, but it may be the solution. In today's world, we have not yet found the way or the model. It is not that we are not looking for it, but we have not been able to reorganise ourselves like others, who were left behind at the beginning but possess great power today. The wound of 1948 was very deep, and the subsequent defeats have eroded our confidence and prestige and discouraged us in the face of possible new major projects. We want to give you, Secretary-General, our confidence, but we want to make clear that, for everything to get off to a good start, this noble journey must begin with a creative and definitive solution that would give birth to the Palestinian State, culminating in an indisputable peace process that would seal the new coexistence in the entire region. You will know how to achieve this. But if we aspire to something greater, a global political governance, a new political architecture of the world, it may well be possible to find a way to settle disputes and build peace. May God enlighten you and may Allah help us all.' With these words he ended his speech, leaving the rostrum slowly and with emotion.

And then the representative of Mexico took the floor, speaking on behalf of a large group of countries of America.

'Mr Secretary-General,' he began with an affectionate but incisive tone, 'we expect a lot from you, since you have the responsibility of responding to all the warnings as well as the immense possibilities that we have heard in this great auditorium. If we leave aside the conflicts, the petty quarrels and adventures of one against the other, we will be able to achieve a better future for all of us, and we can enter horizons of unimaginable prosperity.

'We have all heard all these great things, but it is your responsibility to give final shape to the commitment we must all make. We will not fail you, Secretary-General, be assured of that. But we will not want others to fail you either, nor will we want you to allow yourself to be pushed into a corner by those who do not want a new world to emerge. We must have energy and set out on the new path, now when the modern world has experienced its first global upheaval. The so-called first world has been hit the hardest and has seen the fragility that affects all of us, not just the peripheral countries. Today we are a very advanced global civilisation, and yet a small virus has put us in check. Advances in science and rapid communication have enabled us to defend ourselves, but the failure to act in unison has created gaps, and many live pockets of infection have remained, like a badly extinguished fire. Fortunately, this pandemic has not had the tragic overtones of the devastating pandemics of the past, such as the Black Death, which devastated the old continent, or smallpox, which devastated us with the arrival of the Spanish and Portuguese. Those must have been terrible times, and my region suffered greatly when it was completely decimated. That is why we are very sensitive to the need to consider how to better organise the world and how to better protect ourselves in the future.

'As I said, I represent a region that was ravaged by a pandemic. Today we are a mosaic of differences, although there is much that unites us. Some countries were home to great civilisations like the Aztec, the Maya, or the Inca, while others were a land of migrants.

'Some, like Brazil, have the planet's largest lung of oxygen, while others, such as Bolivia, Chile, Peru, and Mexico, know the harshness of the desert in a large part of their territory. Some are islands and others are landlocked territories like Paraguay. But we are all united, Secretary-General, by a great respect for the evils that humanity can suffer, and we all share an ecumenical conception of our species. We are cultures of peace, cultures deeply respectful of Mother Earth. That is why we are aware that in a disunited world, in a world of national disputes, every great disaster has an open door. A new deadly pandemic could come and again find us without a common protection strategy, or a nuclear conflict could break out and pulverise us. We cannot gamble our existence on the sterile cacophony of national disputes. We need to enter a new era. Today, organisation is the key to success. This is what makes it possible to maximise efforts, create harmony, bring people together, and avoid deadlocks. And today, we must put the power of the political world at the service of citizens. That is why we give you, from this region that seeks a horizon of progress, a resounding yes to your efforts to provide the world with a new, more global and efficient political architecture. Forward, Secretary-General, forward. We will be with you at the front of the pack in this noble endeavour.'

And then the representative of China, a woman of delicate gestures but strong character, took the floor representing the most ancient civilisation, now once again in a position of world leadership. She began her speech by recalling the very long history of her nation:

'It is not lost on anyone here,' she began, 'that my nation was a great empire for more than two millennia, and now we are one again. Other nations have been organised as nations for longer than us, but we alone have endured in leadership. Our eclipse has been only temporary, caused by the West's voracity and desire for expansion. For more than two millennia we have accounted for more than a third of the world's wealth. And we have accounted for it year after year, with no ups and downs. And over such a long period we never aspired to world domination. We like our land, and we don't need new territories or dominions to feel fulfilled. We never left behind the art of war, but it was more a cautious attitude towards possible invasions than an ability to be used for world domination. Thus, we built the Great Wall, a work of defence and not of attack, a Herculean work that reflects our determination and which freed us from the constant invasions of our neighbours. When we could have dominated the world—and there was no lack of opportunities—we never wanted to do so. Nor did we even try. At a time when the West was beginning to go out into the open world and was rapidly taking over villages and territories all along the coast of Africa and America with only a handful of men and very few ships, we only made commercial treaties. However, the great explorer Zheng She, under the orders of Emperor Yongle, undertook five great expeditions with more than seventy ships and thirty thousand men, setting foot in all the territories bordering India and ascending Africa along the Red Sea. We like our culture, our land. We have never longed for more.

'Our greatest decline came at the hand of the West. With the so-called opium war, the system collapsed and what had lasted for centuries was undone in a few years. Then we inherited from the West the Marxist dream, which resonated with our people's deep-rooted desire for collective happiness. The furrows of conventionalism had tilled the soil and Marx's seed took root to build a new society. We lived through very hard times, but we recovered. It was the beginning of a deep cut in our millenary history. But the order of the system has allowed us to regain leadership and get out of the deep depression. With the corrections of Deng Xiaoping and Jiang Zemin, the system evolved, opening up to capture the energy that springs from the grassroots while maintaining an essential order that provides a framework for accelerated development. And we are moving forward to regain our long-standing position of accounting for thirty per cent of the world's wealth. Now, Secretary-General, your proposal to move towards a new world governance comes to the fore. A valuable proposal that will require full guarantees that the system will be neutral and secure.

'Our essential trait is to be a civilisation of peace. Since Confucius, the desire for war and confrontation has been replaced by the desire for understanding and the search for harmony and empathy. But we do not want to take any risks. Our history has known the horror of foreign domination and we do not want it to happen again. Many millions have died to free our country from domination, and our security is one of the most precious values that we will never put at stake.

'We can only move towards a system of global governance if we are in the initial nucleus that designs and guarantees this new world architecture. For that, we need to pool all our military capabilities and learn all the secrets of others. We need to simultaneously sign the agreement that will make outer space our common home. We do not want to bend to the dictates of anyone or anything, but we can agree to embark on the path that will lead us to a secure world system, to the consolidation of a well-guaranteed peace.

'We are sorry that this pandemic started at home, though this fatal circumstance may touch others in the future. We wish to help as much as we can to regain the momentum of progress in the world. That is why we extend our hand to the agreement you propose, and that is why you will find in us a great nation ready to strengthen a peaceful world. I trust, Secretary-General, that our willingness to contribute will be appreciated.'

She was followed by the representative of Russia, once the world's second largest military power:

'I, too, will resort to a brief recollection of recent history,' began a man with snow-white skin, a thick build, and a powerful voice, 'to defend our deep reluctance in deciding to lay down our arms and coming to rely on a global understanding. Although we are an essential part of it, the so called "West" has always betrayed us. It is like a strange relationship in which we always offer an outstretched hand, and the West responds with unlimited greed. A greed that is also arbitrary, excessive, and always fed by the possessive instinct of its leaders. And we have always had to field this voracious attitude, retreating and then reacting to make up for what we had lost.

'What had we done to deserve so many invasions? Nothing more than being a rich land. Such was the case with Napoleon. And then with Hitler, with whom we had signed a non-aggression treaty. But he broke it whenever and however he wanted in his own interest. And what had we done to give him cause to renege on what had been agreed? Nothing, absolutely nothing. It was only the dictator's unbridled appetite, the conviction that he could abuse his dominant position at no cost. But our people rebelled, endured, and won on both occasions. And when the Second World War came, we had to play at being great in order to defend ourselves. We had the courage to implement the alternative model to capitalism that the Europeans themselves had imagined. We did not invent a new system. We put into practice the system that Marx and Engels had designed in Germany. And the Second World War caught us in the middle of the process of implementing that system. The end of the war meant that we were the only country with the alternative system alive, which is why we needed a large area of influence and a wide circle of protection because we feared being crushed by the other victorious powers. We had to pretend to be stronger and bigger than we were. We had to prioritise the military to appear to have a capacity close to that of the other great power, even though our economy and research were moving away from the great performance of the West every year. Our system could not function in modernity because modernity is based on decentralisation, on many taking the initiative and inventing, and our system revolved around an all-powerful central authority that wanted to control everything.

'Evidently, this led to atrophy and paralysis. Instead of offering progress and prosperity, it offered frustration and fear. So, we cleverly undermined the system ourselves and made it easier to reintegrate ourselves into the common European history. But when that happened, what did we get? Unfortunately, much less than expected. While we acted nobly, the West acted as victors always do, and we suffered some of its steps as painful deceptions. We were promised a lesser role for NATO if we dismantled the Warsaw Pact and, as soon as we did, NATO grew year after year until it almost reached our borders. And the same goes for the so-called European Common House. Even if at the beginning of the Perestroika, French President François Mitterrand and German Chancellor Helmut Kohl had wanted to bring us back into the central European story, as soon as the Soviet edifice crumbled, silence descended. Europe's priority shifted towards capturing the former countries that made up our sphere of influence while the door was closed to us.

'We are essentially European and, after losing the battle to lead a model of society, we wanted to resume our history with Europe, which is our cradle and our inspiration, but we were marginalised again. All those who were in our orbit were able to reintegrate into this great family, but the door closed just after the last one had passed through, leaving us outside. We accepted it. We have accepted a lot in our history, and this was not going to be the last low blow that came our way, nor the one that was going to defeat us.

'In these difficult times, we have survived with more hope than success, but we have weathered many blows dealt against us. We have held our own in global geo-politics, and we do not want a world order that is used to push us into a corner. Since the disintegration of the Soviet Union, we have trusted the United States too much and the United States has trusted us too little. We have experienced many disappointments and we cannot now continue to trust naively. Only with a world political architecture controlled initially by the largest and with equal power for all will we be able to support it. And it must be done without burning the boats because it will be a difficult voyage and we must prove how well the ship is sailing. We have always done great things in history, and we have never failed humanity. You can count on us,

Secretary-General, but you can also be sure that this time we will be very vigilant. Too many times we have seen the agreements we have signed betrayed. This time we will sign, but we will not be deceived.' And, with a serious, grave face, he ended his speech.

This was followed by the representative of the largest economic bloc on the planet, the European Union. The woman began her speech with a surprising but very true statement. She was sharp, nervous, and well-informed. With precise diction she said:

'We, Secretary-General, are much and nothing at the same time. We are the largest economic region in the world, but, as in Babel, it is difficult for us to understand each other, especially when it comes to doing something big that requires us to act as one. We are full of contradictions and weaknesses. That is our truth when it comes to taking a stand on such an important issue.

'We have been the scene of so many wars and tragedies that we are united in our desire to contribute to all initiatives to consolidate peace in the world. You can thus count on us, Secretary-General, because we no longer possess the expansionist force that has caused so many changes and tragedies. Today our ageing is leading us all to be peoples of peace, who only wish that a good economy reigns and that life does not bring us too many shocks. Unlike many young people on this planet, we no longer have the strength to engage in quarrels and disputes. We did it too often in the past, and we destroyed ourselves too many times. We are on our way to being useless, although we still have a lot left. We are like a patient who has overcome a very serious cancer and is now recovered enough, but not to start a competition with the strength they had before. But our citizens are brilliant in many fields, and a planet at peace, a planet of individuals and not of countries, can fuel our fire and be fertile ground for many contributions. We could not hope more, Secretary-General, that your project would take shape! Rest assured that we will be at your side all the time, and that we will row for you like those who know that this is the only route that can lead to a safe port. Let us move forward, and not wait for a new onslaught of destiny to plunge us into a new disaster. With this pandemic we have learned that we are all fragile and that we need all kinds of intelligence to act quickly in the face of the unknown. Yes, the idea of moving forward into a new world anchored in the concept of One Humanity deserves our full support and recognition.

'And there is an urgent need to act, before memory fades and petty quarrels and specific interests alter the great project humanity deserves.' And, with a dignified and serene voice, she gave way to the next speaker.

It was then the turn of the representative of the United Kingdom:

'Thank you very much, Secretary-General, for giving us the opportunity to make our voice heard,' said a woman with clear diction and a good rhythm to her words. 'Until very recently we were part of the great European project. Today we are no longer, and this, together with our nuclear capability, and the fact that we have contributed the most over the last three hundred years to shaping the international political fabric, it may be of interest to put forth our vision of the world in relation to your proposal.

'Today we certainly live in a world in transition, a very insecure world, which has come to contain all the possibilities of a fateful explosion. The world is like a land strewn with dormant volcanoes. We are aware of this, but as long as they don't erupt, our life can progress. We are among those who think that we cannot be sure that a volcano will not erupt. We are also among those who think that if it does, it may come so quickly and unexpectedly that it is best to be prepared to be able to cope with the damage. To put it bluntly, Secretary-General, we do not believe that the world can enter a period of seamless world peace and guaranteed progress everywhere. Tensions will persist, and so will the risks. And that is why we do not believe in disarmament, but we do believe in arms control in the first phase of your project.

'You will tell us that this is very imperfect, and our answer is that you are right. But humanity's great advances have only come about as a result of profound crises. Is this crisis serious enough? In our view, no, although it is a clear warning and, if we were all smart, we would take it seriously. But we think that the containment of deaths and the relatively mild nature of the pandemic among many of those infected will mitigate its impact instead of constituting a full catharsis towards a collective triumph. We hope this will not be the case; rarely would we be more willing to accept being wrong. Have no doubt that we are on your side and ready to contribute decisively, but we are seriously concerned that it will take greater evils for us to really change and to march together towards the future.' Wishing the Secretary-General good luck and well wishes, she withdrew to make way for the next speaker.

'We,' said the Turkish representative, whom the Secretary-General had then called upon, 'would really like to see your project succeed and the impossible become a reality. We are no longer the great power we once were. We are grateful for the sensitivity you have shown in calling us and wanting to hear our voice. It speaks well of you to have such high regard for the country that has accumulated wisdom throughout history even though at the present time it cannot occupy any commanding position in the management of the common ship. We are living through a difficult interaction of cultures under an accelerated process of modernisation. On the one hand, there is our intense European vocation, which has arisen after the failure of our model due to scientific backwardness. But Atatürk transformed our defeat in a new hope, and we set our sails in the direction of Europe to reach a safe harbour and join their common project. But we have been treated as outsiders. The doors appeared open to us as we approached, but closed when we were about to enter. Without renouncing the hope that one day this will change, as we are living in times of crossing and assimilation of cultures, as the United States has well understood, we have set out to recover a greater presence in our historical geographic space by reopening ourselves to the East. A costly project, but one that neutralises the disappointment caused by European disaffection. This difficult task, however, leads us to know well the pathos that exists in both Europe and the Middle East, and that is why we share the words of the speakers representing these two spaces. The weight of old age is sapping Europe's energy and the weight of conflict is holding back the Arab world. And we, who know the soul of these two great spaces, clearly perceive their convulsions and wonder how they could better unite their forces. But the weight of history makes it difficult to reinvent oneself. That is why, Secretary-General, the project you are proposing, despite our regret that it would mean the progressive dilution of our identity, may be the only one that remains viable. Yes, to our regret because we would all like to be great again, but we had better be realistic. Putting aside our collective egos, let us make possible a model that can bring success to our citizens. Go ahead, do not falter, for we too will accompany you and, with the vision of a people who have been great and hope to be so again, we will be there for you.

We will be among those who will facilitate the entente between cultures,' he concluded and, with sincere thanks, withdrew.

It was the turn of the representative of Israel, who, with determination, made a speech focused on security: 'Distinguished Secretary-General, allow me to be brief and precise and to focus my words on what is essential to us. We are a small country, but with a community that has lived without a homeland for millennia and has suffered the greatest exercise of extermination in history. We have known the horror of man against man like few others. For us, security is the most precious commodity. We do not want to see our homeland disappear or return to the curse of being a wandering people. It is true that there is nothing better than to have the whole of international society as our protector, and your project aims at that, but it cannot be a failed project! Move forward with solid support and without naivety. For us, everything will depend on the way in which security is guaranteed in the world. This will be the component that will encourage us to give you our support. Above all, be realistic, for the path of humanity is full of treachery, horrors, and evil.' And with these harsh and direct words, he gave way to the next speaker.

The representative of India then took the floor to emphasise the necessity of the project, and also its fragility.

A woman with a direct and serious look, gentle in manner but firm in her convictions, began to speak. 'We are the largest democracy on the planet, and we have never been known for imperial behaviour or for seeking power over the world. On the contrary, we have always been a territory with our guard down and many times others have come to dominate us. These have always been nightmarish periods for us. Nothing in this life we see as final, but we are fervent supporters of peace and non-interference in other people's affairs. We will be faithful collaborators in your long journey. It will not be easy, and we are glad that you have taken on the enormous task of fulfilling history. It is indeed what you have to do, but we do not hide from you that it will be a Herculean task. Others might have thought that it is a task for the future and that the future is still far away. It is to your credit that you are living up to the times: difficult times, times of desolation, but also times when we are rediscovering what is essential. This planet is everyone's home and we must begin to act as inhabitants of a single home. We will accompany you, supporting you as much as necessary, but also knowing that we may not reach our destination, so we must not have excessive illusions about our chances of success. This is a difficult world and everything that is good and positive is easily broken, although in the long run the good will triumph. Count on us and start the long journey.' And, clasping her hands together as she bowed her head slightly in a gesture of farewell, she concluded her address.

The representative of Iran then took the floor. Invoking Allah, he delivered a speech of mistrust, but with an outstretched hand of understanding, thereby sowing doubts and hopes in equal measure:

'We are also one of the oldest and most complex civilisations on the planet. Many generations have passed through our vast territory, producing a soul of many records.

'That is why we do not believe in a world in which material progress distances man's commitment to God. We are all creatures who are passing through, and we do not believe that we can erect a fortress that makes us impregnable. A simple virus has shown the extent to which all our progress is anchored in sand and not on rock. The only rock is given to us by Allah and the rest are illusions. That is why we have made a political revolution to stop the secularist drift and reconnect with Allah. We do not share the desire to move forward at a fast pace and without spiritual values, but we are aware of our isolated and distinct position in the world. We will never stop trying to maintain it and that is why we cannot cease equipping ourselves with defensive forces. But it is true that technological advances are penetrating our society and the new generations are communicating more and more using the codes of conduct of the Western world. There is an important struggle to be waged to preserve identities that we hope can be combined with peace rather than with the clash of nations and wars. We are aware of the value of your project, and we will not oppose it if you can assure that you will allow each people to preserve their traditions and uniqueness and that you will focus primarily on achieving security for all, on neutralising the possible outbreak of conflict. May Allah keep you among his protected and may your work be sculpted with the character of peace.' With these concluding words, he gave way to the next speaker.

The representative of Japan then calmly took the floor:

'We,' said a man of small but extremely elegant and measured gestures, 'have a flag representing purity and the beginning of times—white with a rising red sun. We have always believed in the power of science and intelligence, which is why we are the country with the highest implementation of artificial intelligence systems. We have always been a country proud of its identity, combining beauty and precision. We are first and foremost great islands, and we love independence. We could never submit to the order imposed by another great power. It is true that we wanted to be that great power in the past, but we did not succeed, and we regret our audacity. Since then, we have lived with trepidation, for our security depends on others, and a world based on the power of others frightens us. We live in fear of the future because of the fragility of the system and the high degree of uncertainty. Our new generations resent this and some of them live completely enclosed in virtual reality, giving rise to the *hikikomori* phenomenon, known in the West as severe social withdrawal, and communicate less. Moving towards a global governance system now would be a great relief and would lift the spirits of many. Introducing artificial intelligence systems to support it would be brilliant. It would mean heading well into the future. A new government needs new systems. We can assist in this task by helping to design the implementation of artificial intelligence in the new planetary administration. That is why I say to you, Secretary-General, clearly and forcefully, that you have our full support, and we ask you to count on us to develop new methods of government in which big data will be the instrument of good management. Nothing will be easy, but your project is the one that best suits a world that continues to live in peace miraculously, as there are many latent threats accumulating.

'We are a country that is unarmed, but we look on, in silence, at the large number of armaments that others have. We are a country on the ocean, and we watch with fear as the environment deteriorates, causing glaciers to melt and seas to rise. Our concern is deep. Secretary-General, we need a new global direction that will consolidate peace and take on the conservation of the planet. Your proposal gives us a ray of hope.' And, with much modesty, he ended his speech and gave way to the next speaker.

He was followed by the representative of the small countries.

'I, Secretary-General,' said a small man in a golden silk robe, 'come from the smallest country among your members. I represent the small territories scattered across the five continents. We are by definition territories of peace; we defend life without imperial prowess. Throughout history we have always been places desired by others, although we have never desired anything other than to be able to continue our peaceful existence without ever having the appetite to invade others. We have always feared the great powers, and this organisation is a source of pride and security for us. It is the only platform that forces the great ones to listen to us, even if they are neither interested in nor concerned about us. But for us it is important, because we can show the world the strength of diversity and our determination to preserve uniqueness. We fear, and will always fear, the great powers, whoever they may be at any given moment. For this reason, moving towards the horizon of a world government gives us hope to move towards a world of all. We certainly want to accompany you in anchoring this new world political architecture, preventing it from turning into a new form of oppressive power. We envision it as the system that will allow human biodiversity to flourish in all its splendour. A system that protects the singularities within a global complementarity, making them safe from the voracious predators that want to dominate everything. We will be with you from start to finish, and we only ask that we move quickly and that you are not deterred by challenges.' And, not wanting to take a minute more of everyone's time, he closed his folder and promptly descended from the rostrum.

And then the next representative took the floor, speaking on behalf of the vast African continent:

'We,' said a stout, thick-voiced, well-tempered man who spoke with his hands interlocked and rising and falling according to the tempo of his words, 'have never participated in the construction of a world order. We have always fit ourselves into the design of others. In the first two attempts, the League of Nations, and the United Nations Organisation, which today hosts us, we were for the most part territories under the domination of others at the time. Our voice, our sensitivity, has never shaped the world, never sculpted the set of rules that ordered the game. Today we are given the opportunity and we are not going to say no. Our frontiers are mostly artificial, imposed first by the needs of colonial distribution and then by the accelerated process of de-colonisation. The leading nations of the past have encircled us.

'The world has been divided as they wanted, artificially drawing lines on the map. In many cases they have divided us without thinking of the consequences. Perhaps that is why our adaptation to a world of global governance will be less difficult because for us the division into countries is in many cases circumstantial. Above all, however, I would like to point out that we have entered modernity. We are the youngest continent, and our people want progress and are excited by the opportunities that technology offers them. We need the new order to be sensitive to the drive for development, to understand that not all of us start from the same wealth, and that a world of all must be a world in which the least advantaged are supported by the most advanced. Bear this in mind, Secretary-General, so that this new world architecture is born with a strong base of support for those who are lagging behind, so that it is humanity united as a whole that advances towards that horizon of intelligence. We are with you and our young population will be one of your greatest supporters.' And with this resounding affirmation, he gave way to the next speaker.

And finally, the one who had the most power in the world at that time took the floor. In a clear voice, a vibrant and sharp-minded American woman began by recalling her country's commitment to humanity:

'You all know that my country has been the main driving force behind all the projects the world has undertaken to create bodies to consolidate security and cooperation in the world.' She maintained a calm, confident voice as she stared at the audience that was watching her, following her every word expectantly.

'The first world political organisation was born at the

urging of President Wilson. And the second at the urging of President Roosevelt. Both were great men who lived through the horrors of war with great pain. And without the country being directly called upon to participate in either of the two great wars, we went to both of them to preserve democracy and to stop those who wanted to impose an order of terror and domination. And if there is one country in the world that is the melting pot of the world itself, it is mine. For centuries we have been a land of welcome for people from all parts of the world. Our identity is not based on a closed or an exclusive concept of identity, but on principles and rules that are broad and solid, that allow everyone to play and to take part. That is why, Secretary-General, what we have heard here recently and the project you are proposing is in no way alien to us. We represent the possibility of what is being debated today. I want to explicitly mention that, two hundred years ago, we created a political architecture that made it possible to structure a multicultural area in constant growth, when there were no trains, no cars, no communications, and the distances were immense. Why should all of us, now, collectively, not be able to do the same for the whole world? When we adopted the American Constitution in 1787, there were three million of us. Today we are three hundred and thirty million. A hundred times more! Our rules have served as a channel for millions and millions of people of many different origins and races, and the country has not been fragmented or broken; on the contrary, it has become more united and powerful.

'We are therefore aware of the importance of creating rules that welcome and do not stifle diversity. Diversity makes collective life grow, and we are grateful, Secretary-General, that you have called upon us to try to do so globally. For, as I said, if more than two hundred years ago we were able to provide ourselves with rules that have lasted through difficult periods of war and depression and to accommodate all the transformations that society has undergone, how can we not try today to organise the interconnected world in which we live as a whole? To do this we will have to innovate, but innovation is also something we enjoy and something we have proved ourselves capable of.

'But there is a greater problem that we must not ignore from the outset. Human life has an important motor that drives survival and progress, which is called competition. Our Constitution has been sufficiently broad and general, avoiding regulating the life of the people to a great extent, and focusing on establishing basic guidelines to combine coexistence and broad freedom. If we manage to equip ourselves with a world architecture, we will have to know how to preserve the immense diversity of people without wishing to direct their destinies. There will be downfalls for some, great successes for others, and temporary ascents and setbacks for many, but we must accept that life is always uncertain and subject to chance. Rules must exist to mark the boundaries that no one can step outside, but a compact world must not be built. A world that welcomes everyone, yes; a world that blocks those who want to dominate others, yes; but a world that believes in a single conduct, and single progress, linear and identical for all, no. We must be aware of this from the outset.

'And then we have to carefully consider the problem that will test us all; the renunciation of military power. We are on the one hand the leaders and on the other hand those who have fought the hardest for freedom. Without our superior military skills, which we have unfortunately been obligated to use, the world today would perhaps be in a state of defiance or would be subjugated to the whims of a few. Let us not forget that Nazism could have triumphed and opened the door to immense atrocities. In history, there have been winners and losers, and the latter have been disarmed, but precisely because they have known bitter defeat, we cannot eliminate the possibility that without our superior power, new desires to regain greater power would resurface. The crossroads is difficult, Secretary-General, and we cannot give up our military capacity until your project is so effectively matured that our citizens claim it as their own. In the meantime, we must move forward and, as proof of our willingness to begin the journey, we are making you a concrete proposal. If all countries approve the project of moving towards a One Humanity world, we will accept the creation of a Disarmament Council chaired by you, with executive powers, which will progressively reduce arms stocks and strengthen itself until it is able to oversee all the existing military capabilities in the world. At this point, we will see how further progress can be made, but that will be the task of our children and our children's children. We, who are here today, will have steered the ship of mankind towards the safe harbour of non-confrontation. I wish you luck and success in this exciting but also enormous undertaking.' After an applause, she gave the floor to the Secretary-General. The room filled with a great hubbub as all the delegates were free to discuss among themselves the speeches they had heard.

Chapter 23

To Australia

Transforming mobility: The emergence of the Aerial Age

FROM TOKYO, Nour took a direct flight to Sydney, where she landed in the early hours of the morning. The trip had taken more than nine hours and, despite having slept most of the time, her body was numb from being wedged into the seat. 'Too bad, we can't travel at the speed of light yet,' she thought, as she prepared to exit the plane. 'It would have taken only a quarter of a hundredth of a second to get there! We think we are very advanced,' she said to herself, 'but we have not yet passed the Stone Age of air travel. If only we would get there soon, then we would begin to live in another dimension.'

She stepped out of the plane, and the gangway immediately connected her to a fast conveyor belt that took her directly to passport control. A thought crossed her mind like a shooting star, 'I've always liked this country. I'd almost forgotten how well organised everything is.' The perfection of modernity had struck her from the moment she first set foot in Australia a few years ago. She was then fascinated by how easy it was to talk about anything connected with the future. One always thought of tomorrow; the past and even the present were almost unimportant dimensions. There, during the congress where she had presented her book on the new fields of artificial intelligence, she discovered a passion for flying. Margaret O'Connell, the director of that conference, had quickly taken a liking to Nour and had invited her to fly in her light aircraft at the weekend. 'You'll like it,' she said as they arranged to take off early the next day. They took off in a Cessna C40, and for about two hours they flew over wonderful cliffs. It was fascinating to fly over miles and miles of virgin territory! The next day, when Nour was about to fly back, Margaret told her to come back soon and she would teach her how to fly because she belonged to a club of experts who shared a passion for flying. 'Yes,' she said, 'we'll teach you to fly, and you'll fly over a fascinating continent. It's not difficult and it will give you an unequalled sense of freedom!'

She never thought she could do it; Hamburg was so far from Australia! And her days were burdened from dawn to dusk by mounting commitments that piled up endlessly. But the pandemic had stopped that devouring maelstrom of doing more and more, and suddenly, like a clearing in the sky behind a thick storm, the possibility had opened up of spending a few days in Sydney with nothing to do but learn to fly.

From New York she had contacted Margaret who told her that the pandemic was coming under control there. In twelve days, she would start her vacation, and she encouraged her to visit. They would fly across the continent together and she would learn to fly. She knew who could teach her the fastest.

So Nour took the plane from Tokyo and flew to Sydney. Margaret was waiting for her this time in the arrivals hall, and they embraced as soon as they saw each other. It was curious how two people living on opposite sides of the world could feel so close to each other. There was a very positive energy flowing between them, very direct, one might say. 'I've prepared a great welcome for you. I think you'll like it,' Margaret whispered in her ear, unable to suppress a mischievous laugh.

They soon arrived at her house, and Nour marvelled over the fact that it overlooked the bay. Everything was well organised and well connected in Sydney, where life seemed to flow easily. The house was colonial in style, small but cosy, with a clear minimalism very much in keeping with the brightness of the bay. Margaret told her to make herself comfortable and to rest after such a long trip. She added that she would wake her up in the middle of the evening for an early dinner at the aviation club, where she would introduce Nour to her friends, with whom they would be flying for the next few days.

At six o'clock they left for the club, where the city's most adventurous personalities gathered in the restaurant. At the back table were Margaret's friends—Brian, one of the most famous baseball players in the country; Peter, a young banker who managed large private equity funds; Anne, one of the most prestigious facial surgeons in Asia; and Alexander, a highly innovative and sought-after architect with iconic works in several cities. Margaret made the introductions and soon the six of them were drinking and talking animatedly. They laughed over each other's experiences in extreme flying situations and Nour became ever more interested in learning to fly.

'It makes you feel very free. It's seeing the world in the key of the future,' Alexander said at one point.

'I'd love that,' she said. 'Margaret persuaded me to come, saying you'd teach me very quickly.'

'Well, not so fast that you'll leave us behind!' Peter joked.

Anne, making a show of being very precise, then spread out the map of Australia on the table and determinedly set about marking out routes.

'I propose to start by flying over the coast,' said Margaret, 'then Nour will get an idea of the vastness of the country.'

They filled the map with red and green circles serving as starting and ending points of routes, and decided on the itinerary for the next seven days.

'Well, that's all very well,' said Brian, 'but we need to add a bit of excitement! I propose that for six days we ride around the country and teach Nour how to fly, but on the last day we should have a race to get the adrenaline pumping!'

'Accepted,' said Peter, 'And whichever pair wins sets the next meeting.'

They agreed to leave at noon the next day. Margaret would go on Peter's plane, Brian on Anne's, and Nour on Alexander's.

For seven days they crossed Australia from north to south and east to west without stopping. Nour experienced an incomparable feeling of freedom. The vastness of the country was combined with the pleasure of flying through the clear, empty skies. Little by little, she became more and more confident at the controls. Alexander was confident and patient, two valuable qualities in the art of teaching piloting, and, despite a few scares, Nour dared to take off under his watchful eye on the fifth day.

It was a smooth take-off and became the main topic at dinner that evening.

'Tomorrow it's your turn to practice landing and, on Saturday, to win the big race,' Brian said in a friendly but challenging tone. As a baseball star, competition was in his blood. When the final race came down to the wire, that fighting streak would be a big advantage for him.

During the days of peaceful flight, Nour discovered

the incomparable beauty of Australia. Endless forests, immense deserts, well-organised cities like small points of subtle life in the ocean of nature. A prodigious human life in the middle of nature.

Race day finally arrived, and they all set off early in the morning to race to the finish in Sydney when the weather conditions were at their best. Everyone flew at maximum tension, but only Brian and Anne dared to climb to the altitude limit to get less wind friction and then execute a direct landing without wasting too much time on the approach. Alexander, feeling Nour's skin prickle, chose not to risk it and completed the flight without taking that big risk. All in good spirits, they celebrated Brian and Anne's victory with a lunch that was also a joint farewell for the six of them, although during the flight Alexander and Nour had agreed to have dinner together that night. They had enjoyed seven days of common experiences and adventures combining fun and hard training, and it was time to relax and celebrate.

On the way back to Margaret's house after lunch, the two friends talked about how great the group was.

'I've really enjoyed myself,' Nour said. 'You've been very generous in inviting me.'

'I'm glad it went well, and that you've learned to fly in such a short time,' Margaret replied.

'Alexander has been very charming and has taught me very well,' Nour continued, and after a pause, she added, 'You know what fascinated me so much? As we were descending, we saw in the distance a great cloud of starlings swooping right and left and rising and falling, almost blocking out the sun with their dark cloud. It is truly impressive how these birds can fly together in an almost compact way doing the greatest pirouettes in the sky without even touching each other. Not a single crash! Their flight was perfect and daring without collision. That has stayed with me.'

'I understand, because I too find them fascinating every time I come across them,' Margaret confirmed.

They continued talking about the incredible mobility of the birds until they reached the house. Once there, the two went to rest for a while. Then, early in the evening, Nour left for the club to meet Alexander.

He arrived dressed casually. The next day was the start of a week of hard work, and after getting Nour to learn to fly quickly, he felt euphoric. He wanted to enjoy this last day of vacation as a triumph. They ordered two Campari and sodas and reviewed the countless amusing anecdotes of the past few days. When this was over, Nour introduced the subject of starlings.

'You know,' she began, 'I'm fascinated by the way those birds never collide, how they play with fearlessness and freedom in the sky without ever having any mishaps. And sometimes there are tens of thousands, even millions, in a flight that is as compact as a cloud! While we send airplanes on fixed routes, one at a time and with large gaps between them. We are truly still in the Stone Age of aviation, don't you think? Do you think it's possible that one day, human air traffic will be like that of starlings, with a sky full of traffic, occupying all the space without fixed routes, with millions of individual aircrafts flying at the same time, almost skimming over each other, and never having an accident?' she asked, looking at him with a mixture of expectation and enthusiasm.

'I don't doubt it,' he replied with determination. 'The future is in the sky, Nour, and this will be the great transformation of our century. The great collective traffic of trains, cars, and buses limited by the weight of terrestrial infrastructure...all this has an inevitable expiration date. It's too rigid, it's like the landline telephone compared to the mobile phone! Who can think of calling someone on a landline number today? How will you know if they are there, or able to take the call? Nobody in our generation works like that anymore. The same goes for land transport. Its development has made great progress, but from now on, air transport will rule the game. If you let the horses loose in disarray, they run over and crash into each other, and so do the crowds if you let them loose all at once. On the other hand, you will never see any bird act this way. It is the safest medium, and man, having achieved his dream of flying, must do it as precisely as the birds. This will give us great freedom. We will no longer have to leave cities through narrow streets and limited roads.

'We will no longer have to be aware of timetables and rigidities. In the future, all planes will be powered by the sun and wind, and small drones, controlled by artificial intelligence systems, will become the instrument of freedom for every individual. Today the leap is to implement the autonomous car. If we accept driving at 100 kilometres per hour on roads with dense traffic and cliffs on both sides of the road, why wouldn't we accept going in a small autonomous plane, a drone, flying in a clear sky? The autonomous car will be the norm in a few years and the autonomous plane in just a few more. This, combined with its vertical take-off, will revolutionise the way we move. The future is in the sky, and it won't be long in coming, and this pandemic, by jeopardising everything that is collective, will accelerate it,' he told her in conclusion.

She was impressed by this man's confidence in the future, by his precise way of explaining something so important and life-changing, with the tranquillity of someone who speaks with confidence and doesn't need any chorus to validate him. Alexander explained that complex subject with such simplicity and firm conviction that there was little room for doubt. They asked for more drinks, and she then asked him to continue speaking about his vision of the future of humanity and the potential dominion of the sky.

'Look, Nour,' he said, 'everything will change in the future because of the revolution of air traffic. Who do you think will put out the big fires in the forests in the future? No longer will it be the ground firefighters who have served so well in the past!

'Large fires will be fought with drones that will be able to get closer to the flames than anyone else and work tirelessly, without distinguishing between night and day. They will fly self-regulating directly in relation to each other, like birds do. Or do you think that the thousands of starlings flying in flocks could do all these incredible pirouettes in the air remotely controlled from some manned post? Forget it! They have radar, complex algorithms in their brains that regulate their interrelationship. The same will soon happen with airplanes, drones and everything we humans move in the sky. And this is where the great potential, the great contribution of artificial intelligence comes in.'

'This field holds great promise,' Nour replied. 'If we really manage to move through the air individually, as we have done on the ground with cars, it will open a new stage in the life of humankind. And artificial intelligence will play a key role in this. Only machines can arbitrate perfectly,' said Nour with authority.

'And,' he added enthusiastically, 'flying will become the most sustainable means of transport as soon as systems are developed to power planes with hydrogen because then they won't produce any emissions. Aviation, Nour, is the future: it needs no infrastructure except for take-off and landing; it has no fixed impact on nature; it will become completely safe; it will soon be pollution-free at no cost, thanks to clean energies, and it will allow us unlimited flexibility.'

Then the waiter came to bring what had been prepared for them on the terrace for dinner.

As they took their seats, Nour's mobile rang repeatedly with incoming WhatsApp messages. They sat down and Nour glanced at the phone. She had messages from all her siblings marked urgent. She told Alexander that she had to go to the toilet for a moment so she could read them calmly. When she opened the first of the messages, her soul froze. It was from her brother Jamal, and it said:

'Dear sister, I hope you are still well. Unfortunately, I have bad news. Dad died last night. Death caught him sleeping and he did not suffer, but his absence is already immense. We have set the funeral for as late as possible, for thirty-six hours from now, which is the latest they will allow us, so that you can get here. I love you. We are all together in this great sadness.'

'What?!!' she said to herself, 'Dad's dead?! Oh, how awful! It's not possible, it's not possible, it's not possible, it's not possible...' She took refuge in a corner of the bathroom and wept bitterly. In a few seconds, she felt very acutely that her father would not be with her again, that a part of her life was gone forever.

When she had calmed down a little, she returned to Alexander. Seeing her red eyes and her deep sadness, he gently asked her what had happened. She told him the news without being able to hold back her tears again. He then said, with some emotion, a short but sincere sentence: 'I am truly sorry. I know how hard this time is for you and how dizzying it is to receive this news,' and he let her slowly recover as her spirit wandered through memories of her father.

Alexander understood that she would not be in the mood to eat. He got up for a moment and explained to the maître d'hôtel that something serious had come up and they had to postpone dinner.

The maître d'hôtel told him not to worry and that he hoped everything would be all right. They left the club, and Alexander thought it would be best to invite Nour to his house so that she wouldn't feel alone at such a delicate moment. It was a cheerful house, open to the bay, and there was some nice art hanging on the walls. There was no shortage of Andy Warhol paintings, Newton photos and Pollock originals. To the left of the foyer was his desk in leather, full of sketches of original houses. In the living room there were huge floor lamps and wide sofas from which you could look out over the sea. He didn't want to leave Nour alone after the painful shock of the news she had received, so he invited her to listen to some quiet music while the sun set and the sea turned a pastel blue. He put on Brahms's Intermezzo Op 118, No 2, played by Grigori Sokolov. It was one of his favourite pieces because of the way the great Russian pianist took on the same musical sequence from different angles. Just as space takes on a personality of its own in Velázquez's *Las Meninas*, time became eternal in the hands of that great pianist. Nour was assailed by memories of her father when he used to play with her on Sundays, in bustling Damascus. The beauty with which Sokolov approached Brahms gave her peace of mind, while the waters of the harbour slowly absorbed the sun into the dusk. Alexander had let her pass through this difficult trance in the utmost privacy and, so as not to disturb her, had withdrawn to finish some projects in his office next to the entrance. When night fell, Nour came to see him, asking if he had thought about how he would face death.

'It makes me dizzy,' he said. 'Because I don't have children, when I do think about it, I don't think of the consequences for others, I think only of myself. Will I disappear forever, or will I become some kind of unknown energy? I often tell myself that we are here as physical beings, but perhaps we are much more than that, and we live on as energy. When my mother died, I began to think seriously about this subject. Although she was presumed dead in the early hours of the morning, I had the impression that she only really left when I arrived to watch over her. It was already noon, and she had a slightly petrified smile on her lips. I held her hand, and then I felt her spirit depart. Although her heart had gone a few hours ago, she still retained a halo of life. Only after that singular moment, after I held her hand, did her face definitively cease to be animated and a shadow came over her completely. It was then that I thought that in addition to our physical reality there is perhaps another energetic reality that inhabits us and that perhaps has a cycle of existence different from that of our temporary shell.'

'What you're saying is very interesting,' Nour replied, 'and it gives me a lot to think about.'

The two of them talked about death and life until dawn. It was a very hard day for Nour, and Alexander knew how to accompany her to the depths of her soul, to the registers of doubt, pain, and the unknown.

As it was about to get light, Nour told Alexander that she was exhausted and would take a nap on the sofa, but before going to sleep she asked him if he had ever been to Syria.

'No,' he said, 'I've never been to the Middle East. Zara Hadid invited me many times to stay with her and to work together, but I never found the occasion. Then, after her death, I have never known anyone in the region... except you, now.'

'You'd like it,' Nour told him. 'You'd discover the intensity in people. It will suit you well. It's a world of great personality,' she said. Then she added, 'You taught me to fly. I will help you discover the most beautiful things in the Middle East. I'll return to Hamburg, and whenever you want, we'll meet in Cairo. After I introduce you to the wonders that you must not miss—the Valley of the Kings and the great pyramids of Giza—we'll go on to Beirut, Damascus, Jerash, Petra, and finally the great deserts of Iran.'

'All right, we'll do that, but rest now, it's been a difficult day for you,' he said before he left her lying on the large sofa in the living room.

Theirs had been the quiet meeting of two souls that had come close together without intending to, like two well-written musical fragments that progressively intertwined. It was the beginning of a slow walk together, leading towards the future. It tasted of deep mutual understanding, over a long journey.

After ten o'clock the next day, Nour woke up. A strong smell of coffee filled the room, making the awakening more pleasant. When she opened her eyes, she saw Alexander sitting next to her. He had brought her a light breakfast with the coffee still steaming.

'This will do you good,' he said before giving her an affectionate kiss.

She took his hand tenderly and, with all her heart, said to him:

'Thank you for yesterday. It was very important for me

to feel accompanied.'

And, in small sips, she began to drink the coffee. Then she looked out over the bay and thought, 'It's amazing how life is never linear but evolves through great crises and great hopes. It took my father's death for me to discover the depth of a soulmate. What a conjunction of intense moments.'

He then told her that he had been talking earlier in the day with Margaret, who was very sorry about what had happened. Then Margaret had called to tell him that she had found a flight back to Hamburg that night and had booked it. 'You're both wonderful,' Nour remarked. 'Thank you for taking such good care of me,' she said warmly.

That same night Nour was on her flight from Sydney to Hamburg. Margaret and Alexander accompanied her to the airport and cheered her up. The farewell was short, but affectionate:

'Write to me as soon as you get there,' Margaret told her as they melted into a big hug.

Alexander gave her a very affectionate kiss and, looking at her deeply, he said:

'When you have everything arranged, start preparing for our trip to Egypt and the marvellous places you will have me discover!'

The Lufthansa flight took off over the opera house and the bay, and headed for Doha and from there to Hamburg.

It was a long flight. She took advantage of it to put in order the notes she had been taking during the long, long trip, with the ideas and projects that had arisen.

She had painstakingly translated her experiences into data, for she was eager to see how an artificial brain would process what she had learned and how it would solve the huge tasks of world transformation that had been emerging. The moment was ideal for putting together a different future. The virtual had taken on great momentum and the debate on new ideas had multiplied exponentially. It was time to organise this great potential for the future because after surviving the serious setback, their generation was called to enter the age of intelligence. They could not lose momentum.

She finally landed in Hamburg. After dropping off her belongings in her apartment and taking a quick shower, Nour joined her siblings in the mortuary, where her father's coffin was still open so that she could say her last goodbye before he was taken to the crematorium. The funeral was scheduled for the afternoon, and she wanted nothing more than to hug her brothers, kiss them, cry, and to be with them as one in such a difficult moment.

They were sad but serene. Their father had been very present in their lives. His strong personality had given them all the security they needed to get through so many difficult moments, and now the vastness of their loss was great. The blow had been even harder when death had come unannounced. But there was no choice but to go on. One after another they detailed how Rachel, the woman who cared for their father, had called them in tears when she discovered that the doctor, as she called their father, did not go out for breakfast and, when she opened the door to the room, she found him lifeless on the bed. She didn't know what to do and asked them to take care of everything, and they did. Ahmed did everything he could to delay his removal from the mortuary, so that Nour could arrive to say her last goodbye.

Emotional, she went to the small room where her father's body lay with a serene face. He was surrounded by flowers, and a white cloth covered his body. It was a long and silent farewell of fixed gazes. She was aware of the importance of seeing him for the last time and wanted to absorb all that he had embodied. So many intense and unique days were leaving with him that an unforgettable emptiness opened up in Nour's soul! She cried again and, after recovering, returned to her brothers to leave together on the way to the crematorium.

The evening wore on, and when the ashes were given to them, they went to supper. The three of them asked her to tell them the essentials of the long journey. At the same time they would acquaint her with the difficult social situation into which Europe was slipping because of its lockdown.

She told them what she had thought about future

projects in the desert, the new role that islands would have in the world, the discovery of the new dimension of nature, the revolution in urban planning and settlements, the geometric progression of medicine, the future of mobility by air, the new economy based on intelligence, and so on and so forth. She added in a hopeful tone: 'And, moreover, I believe that I will soon be adding an exceptional travelling companion to my life.' Everyone wanted to know more, and she told them how she had learned to fly a plane in Australia, and how Alexander's confidence and maturity had made an impression on her. And she was particularly excited to meet him soon again.

Shivering slightly, possessed by the fragility of the moment and the feeling of entering a new phase of her life, she said to her brothers: 'The world is going to become more intelligent, but also more distant from each other because the pandemic has interrupted human contact and closeness. Finding a life companion is going to be extremely difficult. I think I have found him, and that gives me a lot of strength to face the future with hope. He and I are going to Egypt soon and then I'll be able to tell you a lot more,' she concluded with a certain mischievousness, leaving them on tenterhooks.

They finished dinner and escorted her home. She settled herself comfortably and sent the message she had promised Margaret. She looked at her bookshelf, at the various pictures displayed there, and got up to look at one that she had been given of her and her father when they arrived in Hamburg. She was five years old in the photo and her eyes were fearful. It was amazing how much her life had changed since then. And her father, who appeared in the photo with all his energy and confidence, was no longer there… 'Life is so grand but so fragile at the same time. We'll have to think quickly about the future so that we don't miss our chance to improve it,' she said to herself with a certain nostalgia.

Margaret texted her back from halfway around the world, and Alexander sent her a supportive emoji, wishing her a safe arrival and reminding her that he was ready for Egypt. 'It's good that life doesn't stand still and that it allows us to reinvent ourselves like a phoenix,' she thought. 'Hopefully the world will do it too.' And then she wished that the dream of that night could take her to the final chapter of the great assembly that was to draw up the future architecture of the world. And so it came to pass.

Chapter 24

Charting The World's New Political Architecture

THIS TIME, Miquel Barceló's magnificent dome looked more powerful than ever in the great hall of the Palais des Nations. Its colours and stalactites glowed with electricity as if they knew the importance of the moment. Nour found herself seated at the end of the middle row and waited impatiently, like the rest of the auditorium, for the man they expected to be able to do everything, who was now going to present the final conclusions after having listened to all the speakers. This was the decisive moment, and the expectation was enormous.

The Secretary-General entered with his characteristic humility, aware that he was acting as a catalyst for what was emerging in the world and not as a new Messiah. Humanity, in the broad sense of the word, was taking the reins of its destiny, and it was up to him to put the new code of coexistence in black and white. The world was clamouring to organise the game with new rules to begin a new voyage of progress that the great pandemic had shown could not be postponed.

'Today,' the Secretary-General began, 'we stand before a decisive day for the world. We have arrived at this day not at the conclusion of an atrocious struggle, like we did in 1919 and then in 1945, but rather because we have been able to understand our enormous fragility after the cruel but clear warning brought by the great pandemic. It was only by announcing the devastation it could bring that the world was brought to a standstill. In the face of a chaotic virus, we have seen the potential for death and destruction that we could suffer and our inability to react to it successfully. We have realised that we must reshape the world's political architecture to prevent a major social and economic earthquake, whether it be the war of a new generation or a deadlier pandemic. A new crisis could bring down the whole of humanity in an instant, just as, during an earthquake, the earth swallows the tallest building like mere dust in front of our helpless eyes. Today we will sign the manifesto of the new world political architecture, driven by intelligence and not by the capitulation of foolish losers and visionary victors. This time it is humanity that is forging ahead using its intelligence, understanding the message it has received and betting on its future. I am honoured to be able to give shape to what the whole world is crying out today, from the bottom up.

'In recent years, the power of individuals has grown and collective power has seemed to lose predominance. This has led many to think that political power was in decline, and conspiracy theories have multiplied as the atrocious pandemic spread. But I want to say loud and clear that what we have experienced in recent years was not so much the disappearance of collective power as it was the multiplication of centres of power. This has made the exercise of power more democratic. The power of the future must be in the hands of each individual under a global political architecture that gives security to all. And our responsibility is to organise this space so that this immense decentralisation of power leads to the unlocking of talent and not anarchy.

'We must establish a new order that allows the whole of humanity to interact in harmony, as happens in nature with its millions of species. That is why we are gathered here and why we proudly want to exercise self-rule globally. Not to run the world, but to design the rules that will allow a new, constantly self-regulating world to flourish and evolve. So far, I think we have done a good job. The Security Council has been able to channel certain conflicts. We have given ourselves the Sustainable Development Goals, and we have created a concrete agenda, the 2030 Agenda, to address the most pressing global challenges in an operational way. Today we must go further, and enter a new organisational phase as humanity.'

At that moment a deep sigh could be heard in the auditorium. The six hundred delegates had followed the Secretary-General's words with undivided attention, and now it seemed that he was going to take his speech up another notch. There was a pause that released tension and brought new energy to move on to the next phase.

'Today, we have witnessed why we can no longer hold back and why a new global political architecture is imperative. The data, ideas, and experiences recounted by the speakers preceding me have been so compelling that we are aware that the choice is between erecting this new edifice and giving wings to the potential of humanity, or continuing to sit on a powder keg that will eventually lead to mass destruction, putting an end to any chance of being one of the great civilisations of the cosmos. Let us avoid perishing horribly because of our disagreements! The most important thing, then, is to set the course well, although the arrival time and the stages of the journey must be seen as variable and modifiable. But not the course. A degree of error means never arriving at the destination. An exact course guarantees arrival, even if the journey involves detours and storms.

'Today we must establish a stable world order for all. And this can be based neither on the balance of nations nor on the wisdom of one leader. Both options are too fragile for the wonder of the future. States, by definition, are made up of groups of people and every group tends to strengthen its signs of identity by creating contours that rub up against those of other groups. Like stones that rub against each other and cause fire, one day the friction of cultures and civilisations will cause humanity to burn. And leaders, having played a crucial role when knowledge did not flow easily to all, are also a way of directing progress that contains too many risks. The perception of a being will always be very limited and they will not fail to harbour some shadows, no matter how enlightened they are. I understand the fears of some, their different visions, for we all come from different starting points and have progressed through different processes. But the pandemic has overtaken us all, and we must cross the river. It is important that we create the new order for all human beings.

'An order that defines the playing field with clear rules, that strengthens and gives security to the common dynamic. I, therefore, urge everyone to set the course today. The time has come to be concrete and to start building the path towards that world of united humanity to which all speakers have referred. My proposal consists of five points, which I present to you as the pillars of the new edifice. They are five points which, if adopted, will then be developed in detail by the General Assembly.'

At this point there was total silence in the room. The great moment had arrived, and everyone knew that what the Secretary-General would propose would have consequences for the future. Under this atmosphere of maximum expectation, he presented the five points that would govern collective life from now on. With conviction, and using institutional language to give them the solemnity that they deserved, he went through them, point by point.

- The decision is taken by all existing States to gradually dilute national consciences in favour of the concept of one humanity. The priority will be to form citizens who are considered for what they know how to do, for what they contribute to others and for what they contribute to the enhancement of human dignity.
- The backbone of the new world order will be human rights. The Human Rights Council will become a prominent body of the new world government that will legislate and enforce the development of these rights.
- Existing conflicts have a reason for being and can by no means be ignored. They are the result of deeply rooted circumstances and interests. They derive from those dimensions which, although undesirable, are irremediably human because they are in all of us—greed, envy, hatred, and the will to dominate. But today, we have decided to overcome them so that they do not cloud our new path. We will therefore create the World Court of Political Arbitration, which will establish the solution for each of the existing conflicts. It will be composed of the last fifteen living Nobel Peace Prize laureates, and its decision, taken

on a case-by-case basis by a qualified two-thirds majority, will be binding. As a collective body, we will ensure its implementation and, leaving the disputes in the past, the world will be able to move on to the new stage.

- The Security Council will become a permanent organ of global governance, expanding to twenty-five members. The current veto-wielding members will no longer have veto power but will retain their permanent membership. The council will create the first global administration to execute initiatives that identify new development paths, and will operate with restricted human teams assisted by advanced artificial intelligence systems. Its effectiveness will progressively demonstrate that its competencies must grow to eventually replace the Administrations of the States.
- The Supreme Defence Authority is established, which will have control over all military arsenals. It will take measures for their progressive dismantling, and will ensure that all military power is for the benefit of mankind.

'As a sign of the new era we are beginning today, the name of the present organisation will change from "The United Nations" to "The United Humanity Organisation". Within a month, the General Assembly will meet to elaborate the principles we are adopting today, and to set us off on this new path.'

The room was full of all kinds of emotion. There was rapturous, enthusiastic applause—applause not only of admiration for the intellectual capacity of the Secretary-General, but also polite applause and contrite or uneasy faces, but there was no veto, no one dared to break the magic of that momentous day. And the proposal, with no dissenting vote, was approved. Much would have to be done in the future, but at least it had become clear that an era was closing, and that there were steps to be taken to move forward into the future.

***

The light of the new day began to filter through the windows of the house, and Nour began to lazily wake up. The dream was over, leaving her with a deep satisfaction. What she had heard filled her with hope.

She tossed and turned several times in bed before getting up, still going over how much she had to do from now on. She could clearly see the extent of the transformations underway, and also that the match was not yet won. The new world was not coming as an inexorable dawn, but as a possible horizon towards which it was necessary to move.

'We are on the threshold of a new territory. We must all have the courage to enter it, and inhabit it with wisdom,' she imagined. The future was certainly open, and the cards dealt were good, but the game had to be played by creating a collective movement towards greatness, by gaining momentum.

These thoughts were racing through her mind as she dressed. She knew that the deep wound left everywhere by the pandemic could lead to discouragement and thus to a spiral of confrontation, or it could give wings to the triumph of intelligence to overcome it. A critical mass had to be built up in favour of the positive. It was necessary to create a collective state of mind that would make moving towards a new world its mantra, thus entering the era of intelligence.

Without further hesitation, she got up, prepared a thick Arab coffee to start the day with vigour, and set to work on the conclusions that her artificial intelligence program offered, after cross-referencing the data she had collected during her journey.

That afternoon, she was giving the master class of the new course at the University of New Technologies, which had just reopened, and she wanted to reflect in her speech the magnitude of the crossroads at hand. She marvelled at the order in which the program was laid out, which greatly facilitated her task. The actions were well grouped and so were the conclusions. It was evident that the capacity to create had become exponential, and that the great pending task was to channel well this enormous flow of energy that sprang from every corner. To this end, one strong idea seemed to be emerging insistently—knowledge and initiative should guide all efforts, and a new political architecture had to accommodate all of them.

She went down to the street and took the car in the direction of the university. The filtered light of the early afternoon sun allowed her to modulate her thoughts well. Because of her somewhat introverted nature, she was worried about her ability to persuade the audience to feel, in depth, the transformations that were underway. She should not flinch, she said to herself, she should sharply point out the significance of the moment.

She finally arrived at the central building of the university and resolutely entered the lecture hall, where she was to give the master class that would kick off the new academic year. As she approached the podium, her confidence grew. She arranged her papers on the lectern, looked at the audience, and was impressed by the sense of expectation in the room. Then, in a firm voice, she began her speech, which focused on the value of artificial intelligence and its contribution to new fields of human activity.

But right from the start, she wanted to make clear the importance of the new direction humanity had to take. She clearly emphasised the possible way out of anxiety and uncertainty. 'Today, more than ever,' she said, 'destiny is giving us the opportunity to do something great together. We are on the threshold of a great change that can transform everything, and we cannot lose momentum. We must cross the threshold and enter a new world. With energy, determination, and innovation, we must build a future that will take us into the age of intelligence. There is nothing more powerful than our minds. Let us not doubt that we can do it!'

And then, listing countless examples of possible transformations, she saw the audience's enthusiasm and interest grow.

When she finished, applause echoed through the room, and Nour took a long look at the audience. There were faces that revealed rapturous admiration, others scepticism, some bewilderment, and many, mixed feelings. And as she scanned the hundreds of faces looking at her, she said to herself, 'Many will have thought my vision too beautiful to be true. But fortunately, there will also be those who will say to themselves that it is too beautiful to let it slip away and not make it a reality.'

And, with some emotion, she descended from the podium and picked up the flowers that two students gave her on behalf of everyone.